just some stuff i wrote

just some stuff i wrote

stories

WILLIAM BELL

SEAL BOOKS

Seal Books and colophon are trademarks of
Random House of Canada Limited.

JUST SOME STUFF I WROTE
Seal Books/published by arrangement with Doubleday Canada
Doubleday Canada edition published 2005
Seal Books edition published February 2007

ISBN-13: 0-7704-2974-4
ISBN-10: 0-7704-2974-2

Cover and text design: Kelly Hill
Cover and text image (paper ball): William Bell

Seal Books are published by Random House of Canada Limited.
"Seal Books" and the portrayal of a seal are the property of
Random House of Canada Limited.

Visit Random House of Canada Limited's website:
www.randomhouse.ca

PRINTED AND BOUND IN THE USA

OPM 10 9 8 7 6 5 4 3 2 1

For William Leeson Kavanagh

What's that you've got there?
Oh, nothin'. Just some stuff I wrote.
Can I read it?
I guess so.

contents

The "Scream" School of Parenting 1

The Staircase 17

The Leaves in this Country 43

Apollo and Dionysos 63

Window Tree 93

Chumley 111

The Promise 143

Beer Can Man 177

Acknowledgements 193

the "scream" school of parenting

I'm thinking of starting a Losers' Club at our school. I'll be president, secretary and membership coordinator, all wrapped up in one. I'll let in gangly, zit-speckled boys whose legs and arms have grown faster than their bodies (not to mention their brains), whose Adam's apples bob like golf balls, whose voices moan like cellos one minute and screech like cats the next. You know the ones I mean. They lean against the gym walls at dances, making sarcastic, sexist remarks, and think that farts are funny. The females I accept will be like me, girls who hate their hair, who always feel they've chosen the wrong clothes for the day, who have no boyfriends, no boobs (maybe our first meeting will be about whether there's a connection), no life.

Okay, I'm feeling down. Way down. I just came from a Drama Club meeting where I found out I didn't get the part I auditioned for, again. This time it was Blanche in *A Streetcar Named Desire*. The drama teacher, Ms. Cummings, a dumpy, mousy-haired hag who wouldn't know a good actor if she tripped over one, told me I missed the part because I hadn't mastered the "Nawlins" accent. Really, that's the way she says "New Orleans." As if she's ever been there. The real reason is because I'm small (Mom says "petite") and skinny (Mom says "slender") and my chest isn't noticeable from the audience (Mom says nothing). Cummings rattled on for days before the auditions about how she'd be looking for actors who can develop sexual tension. "You have to drip sensuality," she urged. "This is Nawlins. This is the South—hot jazz, torrid, sweaty nights, passion," blah, blah, blah. I felt like saying, You try to pulse with sexual tension when you're almost sixteen and you've got a body like a rake handle and you can't remember the last time a boy gave you the eye.

Ah, who cares. It's my birthday and I'm going home to get dinner ready. I hope Mom and Dad make it home on time.

I climb the curved staircase, trailing my hand on the oak bannister, pad down the corridor to my room and toss my backpack on my desk. My CDs have been put away, my clothes hung in the walk-in closet. The bed has been made up, my TV and VCR and stereo dusted. I hate this. The cleaning lady has been in here again. I've asked Mom a million times to tell Audrey to stay out of my room.

I close the door and strip down to my underwear, tossing my clothes over my shoulder onto the carpet—take *that*, Audrey. I stand before the full-length mirror. What a disaster. Wheat-coloured hair. A plain, thin-lipped face, like the "before" picture in a makeup ad. A body as straight and boring as a throughway.

"Naomi, I hate you! You're so deliciously thin," Gillian bubbled the other day as we were dressing for gym. "You could be a model!"

For what? I wanted to ask. A Feed the Children campaign? Gardening clothes?

In my shower, as the hot needles of water prickle my skin, I wonder if I'll feel different tomorrow. Some of my friends make a big deal about turning sixteen, but to me the only positive thing is that I'll be taking my learner's permit test soon. Dad promised to buy me a car when I get my permanent licence next year. That'll be great. I won't be trapped in an empty house any more. If only I had somewhere interesting to go. Or someone to go with.

I put the three steaks I took out of the freezer this morning in some marinade and set them aside. I'm planning my birthday dinner for six o'clock, so I have time to make a tossed green salad and prepare three big potatoes to be nuked. To save time, I hung some bunting paper around the kitchen last night. Just as I'm taking off my apron, the phone rings.

"I'm running a bit late, darling, but I'm pretty sure I'll be home on time," Mom says, breathless as usual. I can tell from the hollow rumbling in the background that she's calling from her car.

With my preparations done, I pop a can of cola and take it out onto the deck off the kitchen to enjoy the last warm rays of the sun. The planks smell of sawdust and resin and wood stain. Our house, situated on three partially wooded acres, is brand new, designed and built by my father. It's very secluded—except for the decrepit houses behind us that were supposed to have been torn down a year ago to make way for a golf course. Dad and the country-club developers have been in civil court time after time. The owner of the old houses wants the tenants out but they keep getting delays. Dad's furious, calls them no-goods and welfare bums, taking him to court on free legal aid while he has to shell out real money for his lawyer. He ought to hire my mother, but she's too busy. The view out the back of our house, which should have included stands of young trees, streams and emerald fairways, is still a rural slum.

There are two semidetached brick boxes. One stands empty, waiting for the wrecking ball. The second contains two families. Behind the deserted building a dilapidated shed slumps in the yard, along with an ancient Buick sagging on concrete blocks, two broken motorcycles with flat tires and, believe it or not, an asphalt-paving machine. The other yard is graced with a teetering pile of used lumber, two wheelbarrows without the wheels, a doghouse without a dog and a yellow snowmobile seamed with rust.

Three preschoolers, two boys and a girl, are playing in this yard, yelling at each other at the top of their lungs as they pull a wagonload of stones across the bare, hard-packed ground. "IT'S MY TURN!" "IS NOT!" "I'M TELLING!"—that sort of stuff. These kids learned to communicate from the adults in the house—there seem to be four or five of them—who are honour graduates of the "Scream" School of Parenting. They shout, holler, bellow, whoop and bawl at each other as if deafness was in their genes. Right now, for instance, the mother is sitting by the kitchen window. I can see the smoke from her cigarette curling up through the screen.

"YOU STOP THAT RIGHT NOW!" she hollers.

"WE'RE NOT DOIN' NOTHIN'."

"I'M TELLIN' YA, STOP FIGHTIN'! AND SHUT UP YER DAMN YELLIN' OR I'M COMIN' OUT THERE!"

"I DON'T CARE!"

She doesn't come out. She's too lazy to haul her carcass off her chair.

"I'M GONNA COUNT TO THREE, THEN I'M COMIN' AFTER YIZ! ONE!"

The three brats ignore her.

"TWO!"

"THREE!" I almost yell, just to end the racket, but the kids continue to scream at each other until the girl takes a rock from the wagon and bounces it off the head of one of the boys. The other boy laughs. The screaming intensifies as I get up and step through the patio door and into the kitchen. So much for country relaxation.

It's six thirty and Dad is still at the construction site. He hasn't even checked in yet. I'm watching a sitcom rerun in the family room when Mom charges through the front door.

"Hello, Naomi!" she trills.

Even after a day of phone calls, meetings, tension and deals—she's a lawyer in one of the big firms in the city—she looks attractive, stylishly dressed, her makeup and jewellery understated. Too bad I didn't inherit her looks. She plunks her briefcase down on an empty chair.

"Happy birthday, darling!"

"Thanks, Mom."

"Has your dad called?"

As the word *no* forms in my mouth the telephone rings.

"Hi, honey. I'm just leaving the site now," he says. "See you in fifteen."

In the kitchen, I remove the salad from the fridge and put it on the table, then take out the steaks. Mom is perched on a bar stool at the counter across from me. I wipe the marinade off the steaks and lay them on a platter. Mom is fidgeting, tapping her lacquered nails on the side of her highball glass.

"How was school today?" she asks as she opens her appointment diary.

"Not so good." It's clear she's forgotten about the audition. "I didn't get the part, just in case you're wondering."

"That's a shame, darling. I'm sorry. I know you worked hard on it." She takes a sip of her rye and ginger. "So who's going to play Ann?"

"That was last year, Mom. This year it's *Streetcar*. Sarah Taylor got the part I was after— Blanche."

"Oh, well, Sarah's a nice girl."

Nice if you like stuck-up and obnoxious.

A chirrupy noise comes from Mom's jacket pocket. She takes out her phone and flips it open.

"Yes? Yes, I— Oh, god, I was afraid of that. Yes—"

While she talks I step out to the deck and pull the tarp off the barbecue. One of the adult-male screamers in the other yard is squirting lighter fluid on some balled-up paper and bits of wood piled on a hibachi that's balanced on the end of a picnic table. He seems to be the dominant male of the household—a late-middle-aged scarecrow with stringy grey hair held out of his face by a dirty baseball cap, a gaunt face grizzled with a few days' growth. With a loud *poof* the fire bursts up from his barbecue, forcing him back. He takes a pull on his beer and stares at the smoky fire as if he'd never seen flames before.

Starting our barbecue is a matter of turning the valve on the tank, switching on the dials and pushing a red button. *Pop!* goes the blue flame. I adjust the dials, lower the lid to let the heat build up and go back inside just as the scarecrow begins to bellow at the kids, who are digging a hole beside the snowmobile.

Mom flips her phone closed and puts it down next to her empty glass, frowning.

"What's up, Mom?"

If you're the daughter of a lawyer you have to be able to keep secrets. Mom knows I never ever pass on what she tells me about her cases.

"It's the nursing home action. It looks like we're going to lose—the first round, anyway. Jack is with their lawyers now, trying to work out a settlement."

The Red Pines Retirement Community on the other side of town always seems to be in trouble for code violations. The firm Mom works for represents Red Pines.

Her phone, a little thing, blue with a stubby black antenna, chirps again.

"Yes? Uh-huh. No, no way we'll agree to that. They're bluffing. No, I can't, not yet. Maybe later. I'll call you." She flips it closed. "I think I'll take a shower and get into something fresh," she says, slipping off the stool.

In the other yard, my pyromaniac neighbour seems to have his fire under control. He has been joined by the dumpy woman, another cigarette dangling from her mouth, and two men. The four of them are sitting on kitchen chairs on their porch, drinking beer from bottles and discussing something with a lot of energy. Occasionally, a burst of laughter punches into our kitchen.

I'm tossing oil-and-vinegar dressing into the salad when Dad bursts in.

"Hi, kiddo, how's it going?"

My father doesn't look like a builder. He's small for a man—"Not short, on the lower end of average," he says—slim, with black hair and rugged features. He takes his phone—wood-grain finish, very appropriate—from the pouch on his belt and puts it on the countertop beside Mom's, then pulls an imported lager from the fridge and pours it carefully into a tall, tapered glass.

"What a day," he sighs, a moustache of white foam over his lip. "Sometimes I wonder if those idiots can spell the word *schedule*, never mind keep one." He wipes away the foam with the back of his hand. "How's things with the smartest almost-sixteen-year-old at Woodlawn High?"

"Okay, I guess." I wait, but he doesn't ask. "I didn't get the part," I tell him. "Blanche, in *Streetcar*."

"Shoot. I know you wanted that one badly. Oh well, there will be other roles."

Maybe so, but I won't get them. I'm obviously going to go through life playing walk-ons. The microwave beeps, and I jab each potato with a fork to make sure it's done.

"I'm going to put the steaks on now, Dad, okay?"

"Great. I'm hungry as a wolf."

I take the platter of meat outside and slap the steaks on the hot grill, where they immediately begin to hiss and splutter, then set my watch for two minutes.

"HATTIE, I TOLD YOU TO LEAVE HIM ALONE!"

"I DIDN'T TOUCH HIM!"

"YES, YOU DID—I SAW YOU. STOP THE DAMN LYIN'."

"YOU'RE THE LIAR, NOT ME."

"WATCH YOUR TONGUE, MY GIRL, OR I'M COMIN' DOWN THERE AND WHACK YOU A GOOD ONE."

"BETCHA WON'T!"

The kid knows what she's talking about. The adults holler threats but remain parked in their chairs. Only a nuclear blast would budge them. Or a drained beer bottle.

My watch beeps and I turn over the steaks and set the timer again.

Scarecrow is flipping hamburgers in a cloud of smoke. "SANDY, BRING OUT SOME MORE BEER WITH THE POTATOES."

"ALL RIGHT, ALL RIGHT," comes a

muffled female voice from the house. "I ONLY GOT TWO HANDS, YOU KNOW. ONE OF YIZ COULD SET THE TABLE."

I lift the steaks off the grill with the tongs and turn off the barbecue, then carry the platter inside, slamming the patio door behind me.

At the table, Mom and Dad look anything but relaxed as they cut into their steaks.

"This is delicious, kiddo," Dad offers. "Best steak I've ever—"

A phone chirps. Both Mom and Dad look at the countertop where the two phones rest like little soldiers, ready for action.

"Do you think we could possibly get through my birthday dinner without your little friends over there?" I ask my parents.

"It's mine," Mom says, standing and snatching up the blue one. "Yes?"

"So are there any other parts in the play you can get?"

"Okay, that's a bit more reasonable."

"Not really, Dad. It's basically a three-hander."

"Oh. I've never seen that play. Never liked O'Neill."

"No, we won't budge on that point. We can't."

"It's Williams, Dad."

"Oh, yeah, right."

Mom sits down again. "I'm sorry, Naomi, but I'm going to have to go out later."

"Aw, Mom, it's my birthday. I rented a video and everything, that French flick you guys were talking about last week."

"I know, dear, but it can't be helped. I've got to be there. The whole thing's falling apart."

We eat in silence for a few moments. I'm doing a slow burn, wondering why I bothered to go ahead with this charade of a birthday party to begin with, but no one seems to notice. As if on cue, a phone squeaks.

"My turn, I guess," Dad says. Then, into the phone, "Magee here."

"I'll try to be back as quickly as I can, darling."

"What do you mean, the insulation won't be there in the morning? They promised."

"Can we watch the video later, Mom?"

"Sure, that will be fine. I'm looking forward to it."

"But we can't proceed until the drywall comes. I was hoping to get it up and taped tomorrow."

"Okay. I guess I could work on my project until then."

"Oh hell, you really think I need to come over there?"

"Is that the essay on teenage alienation?"

"No, I handed that in long ago. Got an A, too."

"Wonderful. I'm proud of you."

Dad plunks himself down in his chair. "I've got to slip out for a half-hour or so after dinner."

Mom frowns. "Well, why don't you open your gift now, dear, just in case we're held up?"

The other yard is lit by a spotlight dangling from the clothesline pole. The whole bunch of them are munching hamburgers, sloshing down the beer, yakking and laughing. I sit on our deck in the dark, holding my gift in my lap. It's a portable CD player, pink-pearl finish, with lots of buttons—all the features. It's expensive, a real gem.

The colour is different, but it's the same model Mom and Dad bought me for Christmas five months ago.

I hold it in my lap, my fingers caressing the smooth plastic. In the other yard, somebody turns on a radio.

the staircase

— Okay, I think we can start now. For the record, I am Sergeant Carl Poole, badge number 1875. Case number 09 dash 03. It's May 5, and the location is the principal's office of Hillcrest High School. This interview begins at 1:15 p.m. State your name and address for the record, please.

— Malcolm Henry. 234 Oak.

— That's here in Lakeville?

— Yes.

— Do you know Akmed Khan?

— Not really. I know who he is. He's in my grade.

— That's grade eleven?

— Yeah.

— Do you share any classes with him?

— Gym.

— So you weren't friends.

— No.

— On May 3, during the lunch period, were you in the vicinity of the staircase that leads from the second floor to the lobby outside the library?

— I wasn't right there. I could see it, though. Me and Bo were hanging around my locker at the other end of the hall.

— Did you see anything unusual?

— I saw a crowd at the top of the stairs. Then I heard someone yell, then some girl screamed. That's all.

— Were you near that staircase at any time during the lunch period?

— No.

— What about your friend Bo?

— Nope. We were together the whole time.

— All right.

[tape ends]

TAPE #2

— Just let me get this thing working. All right, I think that's it. Now, you're—

— Jason Popham.

— You're class president. Mrs. Carlucci's homeroom.

— Correct. Look, I'm sorry I was late. Rugby practice went on and on. Coach Dow was mad at everybody today. Had us doing push-ups, laps, you name it.

— We're trying to get to the bottom of the incident that took place on May 3.

— I'll be glad to help in any way I can.

— I'm trying to learn what I can about Akmed Khan. I thought, since you're a class leader, you'd be able to help me with that.

— I'll try. But I don't know him very well. Nobody does.

— Would you describe him as a loner?

— Yes. He keeps to himself most of the time. He doesn't hang out with anyone. That I know of, anyway.

— I understand he's new to the school.

— He started here in September. Moved from Brain, or somewhere. One of those Arab places. Geography isn't my best subject.

— Bahrain.

— If you say so.

— As class president, did you make any attempt to help him assimilate?

— I tried. Once. You know, tried to strike up a conversation. He made it pretty clear he preferred to be on his own.

— So, you would say it wasn't a language problem.

— No, he speaks English okay. He has an accent, a pretty thick one. But you can understand him.

— A cultural thing, then?

— I guess so. I don't know what his problem is. He isn't a joiner.

— Not part of the in-crowd.

— That's for sure.

— Were you in the vicinity of the staircase by the library lobby when the incident took place on May 3?

— No. I was outside with my friends. It was a nice day.

— Is there anything else you can think of that would help in this investigation?

— No, not really.

— All right.

[tape ends]

TAPE #3

— . . . State your name.

— Julian.

— Last name?

— Williams.

— Address?

— 41 North Street, Unit 2.

— You're in Mrs. Carlucci's homeroom?

— Yeah. Look, I don't have to answer any of your questions if I don't want to.

— Where did you get that idea?

— You can't question me without an adult present.

— Quite the lawyer, aren't you?

— I know my rights. And why are you taping this? What's this all about?

— You know about the incident at the library staircase on May 3?

— The day before yesterday. *That's* what this is about. Uh, no, I don't know about no incident. I . . . wait a minute! I wasn't even here that day.

— Where were you?

— At home.

— Were you sick?

— No, I slept in, then I figured, might as well stay home.

— So you were in all day?

— Yeah, watching videos and that.

— Were you with anyone?

— No.

— Phone anyone? Call out for a pizza?

— Yeah, I called a friend.

— Name?

— I don't have to tell you. I don't have to tell you nothin'. I'm leavin'.

[tape ends]

TAPE #4

— For the record, it is May 5, I am Sergeant Carl Poole, badge number 1875. This interview is being conducted in the principal's office of Hillcrest High School. Please state your name and address.

— Gina Tattaglia. 90 Barlow Crescent. Is this going to take very long?

— It depends.

— On what?

— Obviously, on your cooperation. Now, can we start?

— Sure. It's just that I have a meeting, and it can't start without me. The prom committee.

I'm the chairperson.

— I'll try not to hold you up, then. As you know, we're looking into the incident involving Akmed Khan. I'm trying to get some background on his relations with his classmates and so on. Do you know him well?

— No. Not at all.

— Ever talk to him, walk with him when classes changed? Anything like that?

— Absolutely not.

— Why absolutely?

— I mean, well, I just don't know him, that's all.

— I've been told he keeps to himself a lot.

— I guess that's true.

— By choice, do you think?

— I wouldn't know.

— So you can't help me at all in this respect.

— No.

— All right. Let's talk about the episode in the cafeteria on May 3.

— What day was that?

— Wednesday.

— Oh, okay.

— You were at school.

— Of course. I never miss a day.

— Were you present in the cafeteria when the scuffle took place?

— I don't remember any scuffle.

— Miss Tattaglia, I'm told that there is some kind of incident in the cafeteria almost daily. Do you want to reconsider your answer?

— Well, I mean, I guess I was there, but I don't remember any—

— We have several witnesses who say you were not only there but part of the incident.

— Who told you that? Who?

— I'll ask you again, do you want to reconsider your answer?

— Okay, okay, I remember something went on. It was no big deal. It happens all the time, like you said.

—What was your part in it?

— I didn't have a part. What are you trying to say?

— I prefer you to tell me.

— Well, I don't have anything to tell you. Yes, I was there that day. No, I don't remember anything. Now can I go?

— For the time being, yes.

[tape ends]

TAPE #5

— . . . All right, so much for the formalities. Now, Mr. Sedgewick, you were supervising the cafeteria at lunchtime on May 3?

— Yes.

— For the whole period?

— That's right.

— And the lunch break is—what? An hour?

— Give or take.

— What are your duties when you're monitoring?

— Basically, to keep order. Make sure the kids clean up after themselves, things like that.

— Prevent the dreaded food fights?

— For sure.

— Did anything out of the ordinary occur on May 3?

— Not that I recall, no.

— It was only a couple of days ago.

— One day is pretty much like another.

— Were you in the cafeteria the whole time?

— Of course. We're expected to remain until the bell goes.

— So you don't recall any kind of disturbance?

— No.

— How do you supervise? I mean, do you walk up and down the rows of tables and so on?

— That's basically it. Stroll around. Talk to some of the kids.

— Ever take a break?

— What do you mean?

— Well, like, nip out for a smoke? Make a phone call? Whatever.

— I don't smoke.

— So, tell me why you don't remember the altercation that witnesses say occurred on May 3.

— I . . . perhaps I sat down for a moment.

— Where?

— In the cafeteria. I didn't leave. But there's a quiet table near the door.

— How long were you sitting at the table?

— Oh for heaven's sake! I don't know! I had some papers to grade. Reports are due Monday.

— Were you occupied with your papers for the whole period?

— I could have been. Look, you have no idea of the workload.

— All I'm trying to establish, Mr. Sedgewick, is whether or not you witnessed the scuffle in the cafeteria.

— Okay, I heard something. I went over to

see what was going on. But by then it was over. It was nothing.

[tape ends]

TAPE #6

— You are JoLynn Taylor?

— Yes.

— And I have your address correct?

— Yes.

— And you are in Mrs. Carlucci's homeroom?

— That's right.

— How well do you know Akmed Khan?

— Not well at all.

— Ever have a conversation with him?

— Maybe once or twice.

— What about? Do you remember?

— A couple of times, at the beginning of the year, I tried to, you know, just pass the time. Talk about our classes, assignments, like that. But he just blew me off.

— Does anyone else in the class have any kind of relationship with him?

— None that I know of. He's, well, pretty unpopular.

— Why?

— Well, the thing is, at first I kind of felt sorry for him, you know? By himself all the time. It's hard to break in to a new school. Believe me, I know. You never saw him talking with anyone. Not in the halls, or on the way to school, or in the caf. He seemed very lonely. At first.

— At first?

— Then I realized that he wanted to be. He doesn't care about being part of the class, or any of the clubs or teams.

— And that makes him unpopular.

— I don't think it's that. It's his attitude.

— Opinions, you mean?

— Yeah, sometimes in discussions—Mrs. Carlucci never lets you away with it if you say "I don't know" or "I don't have an opinion." She *makes* you participate. Anyway, he said some things that put me off. That's why I gave up trying to be friendly and left him alone.

— What did he say?

— For instance, it was pretty clear that he has a lot of contempt for us.

— Your classmates?

— No, not just us. Everybody. Society. He seems to think we're all, I don't know, immoral or something.

— Does he give any indication why he feels that way?

— I think it's his religion. He's against drinking, for example—there's nothing wrong with that, but with him it's such a big thing—and he thinks us girls act like prostitutes, walking around with our skin exposed and all. He sure doesn't have any respect for us. Even Mrs. Carlucci.

— You mentioned his religion. He's Moslem?

— Yeah. But it's more than that. I got a couple of friends who are Moslems, and they're not like that. See, it really bugs people if you let them know you think you're better than them. And it bugs them even more if you show you don't care what their opinion of you is. Most new kids try hard to fit in, be part of a group. He doesn't care.

— Were you present during the incident at the staircase on May 3?

— No, I was working on a late essay in the library. I didn't even have lunch. I heard the noise, though.

— Anyone you know see anything?

— Way I heard it, the clique was there. Only them.

— The clique?

— Yeah. You know, the class president and his crowd.

[tape ends]

TAPE #7

— Thanks for agreeing to meet with me again. I just have a few more questions, Miss Tattaglia. But first, for the record, the date is May 7, I'm Sergeant Carl Poole, badge number 1875, and the place is the guidance office of Hillcrest High School. There, now we can start.

— I thought we'd been over everything.

— You said that you weren't there at the staircase when the incident took place.

— That's right.

— We have witnesses who saw you.

— But, I meant, I wasn't there when he fell.

— I think it's time you came clean with me. I should remind you this is a very serious matter.

— You think somebody pushed him, don't you? Is that what you're trying to say?

— Did you push him?

— Nobody did.

— How do you know, if you weren't there?

— All right. I was there. Fine. But nobody pushed him.

— Let's go back to the commotion in the cafeteria that day. You said you didn't remember.

— That's right.

— We have witnesses who put you right in the middle of it.

— Who? Who said that?

— One of the clique.

— The what? I don't believe you. Who?

— It doesn't matter who. Now, I'm asking you one more time. Were you or were you not part of the disturbance?

— Okay, I was close by. But I had nothing to do with it.

— All right, Miss Tattaglia, I'm going to have to—

— Look, what's the big deal? A guy fell down the stairs. It was an accident. I don't see why—

— The big deal is, Miss Tattaglia, that Akmed Khan died thirty minutes ago, and it looks like you are right in the middle of a murder investigation.

— Oh my—

— Now you will wait in the other room until I call you.

[tape ends]

TAPE #8

— Mr. Popham, state your age.

— I'm eighteen.

— You understand that this has become a murder investigation?

— Yes.

— And that you are entitled to have a lawyer with you? Do you wish to call a lawyer?

— Am I under suspicion?

— You must answer my question.

— No, I don't need a lawyer.

— Fine. Now, let's go back over your answers. You said the other day that you were not there when Akmed Khan fell, or was pushed, down the staircase by the library.

— He wasn't pushed.

— So you *were* there.

— Yes, but nobody pushed him. I swear. He fell.

— He was surrounded by members of the clique.

— It's not a— It's not like it sounds. We're just friends. We hang out together.

— What did you all have against Akmed?

— Nothing. That's just it. You're making this sound like we were out to get him. That's crazy. We just happened to be near him when he fell.

— Well, that's not what Miss Tattaglia says.

— What? What do you mean? What did she say?

— I want to ask you again about the incident in the cafeteria the day Akmed fell and— He broke his neck, by the way. Did you know that?

— Er, no.

— You didn't ask about his injuries? Your own classmate?

— No. Why should I?

— In the cafeteria, what was your role in the disturbance?

— I had no role. I happened to be nearby, that's all.

— And what did you see and hear?

— I wasn't really paying attention. Akmed was in the middle of a group of kids and there was some pushing and yelling. That's all I remember.

— Well, Miss Tattaglia has told us that there was more to it.

— Whatever she told you, she was lying. Ask her about what she said to Akmed.

— What did she say?

— She was taunting him.

— Taunting him how?

— I don't know, I didn't hear. She . . . she leaned down and said something to him, then walked away.

— Then what happened?

— I'm not sure. I wasn't paying attention. I was trying to catch up on some homework and I looked up and I saw her go over to him. She said something to him, and I turned away.

— That's all you saw?

— Yes.

— You weren't curious that your friend, who purported to have no interest in this boy, was suddenly talking to him?

— You make it sound like we treated him like an outcast. It wasn't like that. People talked to him all the time.

— But you suggested she leaned over and whispered something. Something that made him react. You said she taunted him. Did she tease him often?

— No. It wasn't like that.

— What about you? Did you hassle him, too?

— No. Certainly not. Look, the guy was a bore, a snob, he didn't want to have anything to do with us. Why would we bother with him?

— Maybe *because* he wanted nothing to do with you. Because he didn't acknowledge the primacy of your little clique. All the other kids envied you. You liked that. But he didn't. He thought you were a bunch of losers.

— That's crazy.

— At the staircase, where were you exactly when Akmed fell?

— I don't really remember. We were all there, or most of us. In a bunch, like. Akmed was ahead of us. He just sort of fell. Nobody was near him. It was an accident.

[tape ends]

TAPE #9

— . . . because things have changed, Julian. You said you were home all day.

— Yeah, so?

— We have two statements from students who saw you in the cafeteria. Well? Anything to say?

— You said the guy died?

— Broke his neck on the staircase.

— Jesus. I didn't think they'd go that far.

— Who?

— Nobody. I was just thinking out loud.

— Look, Julian, I need for you to drop the attitude you came in with last time we talked. This is about murder now. We think someone intentionally killed Akmed Khan.

— Last time I thought . . . you wanted to talk about . . . something else.

— All right. Let's start over. You were at the school on May 3, at lunchtime.

— Yeah.

— In the cafeteria.

— I stayed home all morning. Slept in, like I told you. I came to school at lunch to meet up with someone. I was there.

— And you saw a fight in the cafeteria.

— I wouldn't call it a fight. But they were hassling Khan.

— Who was?

— The big-shot class president and all his suck-ups. You know—rugby team, dance committee, Students' Council. The Lakeside crowd.

— That's what you call the in-crowd at this school?

— Most of them live in Lakeside. They're a clique.

— Did they bother Khan a lot?

— He was a jerk. I guess he asked for it. But every once in a while one of them, especially Tattaglia, would really get on his case. Goad him, like. They wouldn't leave him alone.

— Getting back to May 3. What did you see?

— It happened fast. Tattaglia walks past Khan. He was sitting alone, minding his own business. She says something to him. He jumps up and goes after her. Next thing you know, the rugby goons have him down on the floor.

— And it ended there?

— Yeah, except . . .

— Except what?

— Popham goes over and messes with Khan's lunch somehow. I couldn't see what he did, though.

[tape ends]

TAPE #10

— All right, Miss Tattaglia. Just a few more points and we'll have to let this investigation take its course. I'm not sure what the Chief of Police wants next.

— What do you mean, "take its course"? I told you everything I know.

— We've been talking to Mr. Popham.

— Jason? So?

— So we know what happened. All of it.

— All of it? All of what?

— I think it's important that, before we go any further, I should inform you of your rights.

— My— Hey! Wait a minute! What the hell's going on here?

— You have the right—

— Stop! Shut up! What are you doing? What did he say?

— to have a lawyer present. I am arrest—

— I said shut up! Look, it wasn't me! It was his idea, right from the start!

— What was his idea?

— The whole thing. It was Jason's idea.

— Let's continue this down at the detachment. [tape ends]

TAPE #11

— It was Gina's idea.

— Just a minute, Jason. For the record this interview is recorded at the 21st detachment on May 10. I am Sergeant Carl Poole, badge number 1875. Present at the interview are the witness, Jason Popham, his counsel—Identify yourself for the record, please, ma'am.

— Margaret Linford.

— And Sergeant Harry Singleton. Go ahead, Jason. What was whose idea?

— The whole thing. Gina came up with the plan, and we went along. It was . . . it was supposed to be a prank. He was so damn high and mighty all the time. You—

— You mean Akmed Khan?

— Yeah. Anyway, you should have heard him, saying we were all inferior, with low morals. He called us . . . he actually used the word decadent. I mean, how pompous, how conceited can you get?

— You wanted to take him down a peg.

— Yeah, that was it. That was all. It wasn't . . . We didn't . . .

— Go ahead.

— Well, Gina said it would be funny if we could get him drunk. Because he was so death on alcohol and all that. Saying it was a sin. So the bunch of us, we're sitting around one day during lunch, outside, it was a nice day, and she suggested the idea. Somebody said, how can you get a guy who won't drink to drink? She laughed and said it would be easy.

He always sat by himself in the caf. He always drank a can of root beer, like a kid in elementary school, with a straw. She would find a way to get him to leave his place for a few minutes, then I would pour some vodka into his root beer. You know, because you can't smell it or taste it. So that day, she walks by and leans over and says something to him. I don't know what. Something dirty, probably. He blushed like crazy and his eyes bugged out. He jumped to his feet and ran after her, and then grabbed her by the shoulder and spun her around. Can I have something to drink?

— Sergeant Singleton?

— Sure. Be right back.

— Go ahead, Jason.

— Well, I guess Gina wasn't expecting him to grab her. She let out a shriek and slapped him. Then a couple of guys, they're on the rugby team with me, they wrestled him down. When they saw the teacher monitor coming, they let him up and took off fast. So did Gina.

— And you accomplished your mission?

— Yeah, I got a good four ounces into the can. When he came back to his spot he looked even madder. He gulped most of the pop down in one shot, gathered up his lunch stuff and left. We all sort of followed him, hung back, like, so he wouldn't notice. He went outside and sat on one of the benches by the field. Then when the bell sounded he headed back in. He was wobbling a little by then.

— Here's your drink. Water okay?

— Thanks. So, anyway, we followed him up to his locker. Then we sort of . . .

— Do you want to take a moment, Jason?

— I want to . . . to get this out. We, we stood around him and made fun of him. Insults, like. Saying stupid things. Allah this and that, and shouldn't he be home, grovelling on his prayer mat. He slammed his locker shut and pushed through us. He was weaving pretty good by then and he had a funny look on his face like he couldn't figure out what was wrong with him.

We followed him down the hall, hounding him all the way. He reached the top of the stairs and he just . . . he just . . .

— Take it easy, Jason.

— He seemed like he was trying to walk out into thin air. Like there were no stairs there at all, as if the hallway continued. And he . . . just dropped down out of sight. Disappeared. Somebody screamed, but by then we were all moving fast in the opposite direction.

— Take your time. There's no hurry.

— I called everyone together and we made sure we got our story straight. We knew somebody would be asking us what happened. Look, we didn't want to hurt him. It was an accident. If only . . .

— Only what, Jason?

— If only he'd been more like us.

[tape ends]

the leaves in this country

Mrs. Perkins awoke to the double tap of cat feet on her duvet. Without opening her eyes, she reached out her hand and ruffled the fur along Sadie's arched back, earning a contented purr.

Hello, old girl. You want your saucer of milk, don't you? Well, be patient. I can't get out of bed as quickly as I used.

The cat leaped indignantly to the floor as Mrs. Perkins drew her knees to her chest, pushed aside the duvet and levered herself upright. She pulled on her housecoat, slid her feet into her slippers and slowly got to her feet, her lower back cracking audibly. She made her way slowly toward the kitchen, tying the belt of her housecoat into a bow.

It seemed her joints, especially her feet, were stiffer with every passing day. Look at the way I walk, rocking side to side on club feet like a decrepit old hag, she thought. They'll be after me to use a cane next. Oh well, my back is still straight. I can still hold my head up.

The kitchen was bright with morning sunshine. Mrs. Perkins plugged in the kettle, removed the milk jug from the refrigerator, and poured some into Sadie's saucer before placing the jug on the table. The tea things had been laid out the night before, as usual: the Spode pot and sugar bowl with the sterling silver spoon, the single cup and plate, the crystal butter dish. She'd have to start keeping the butter in the refrigerator overnight. Summer was on its way.

Mrs. Perkins put two slices of bread in the toaster, then padded into the living room to draw the drapes. The rising sun lit the garish white bricks of the apartment building at the bottom of the street, the garbage pails in front of the houses, the cars parked bumper to bumper along the curb.

That seedy-looking man in the triplex, the one who seemed never to wear a shirt, had left the mattress on his lawn again, with the sign on it: $25. Heavens, as if anyone would buy it. Turning the whole street into a yard sale. The entire nest of them in that building didn't care a whit about how the neighbourhood looked. Mrs. Perkins made a mental note to phone the city again and complain.

She remembered the way it used to be, the street canopied by elms, the *clip-clop* of the horses that drew milk wagon and bread wagon, every car in its own driveway. Course, in those days no one had two cars. Some people didn't even have a car at all. And you knew your neighbours then. You could send the boys three blocks away to the park to skate or play baseball without worrying. You could see the lake from here, and Mrs. Bunn's house and crabapple trees. When the boys were children they climbed those trees. But they had torn down Mrs. Bunn's lovely bungalow and chain-sawed the fruit trees to make room for that monstrous white apartment building.

The boys. Grown now. Men. Simon in Vancouver and Andrew somewhere or other in the Caribbean.

Her reverie was broken when she heard the toaster pop. She returned to the kitchen, made the tea, sat down with her toast and butter.

Today she would work in the potting shed for a while, repotting her houseplants, then make a start on the garden. The frost was long out of the ground. Summer already—well, not quite. The beginning of June, then. The years pass so quickly, she mused, spreading butter on her toast, and yet each day seems to drag.

June, she said out loud. Her birthday, in fact. She thought about the boys again, hoping that Simon would call. Andrew wouldn't, she was sure. How different they were. Simon a successful stockbroker, a good head for business like his father, and far more successful than poor Gerald ever was. Still, Gerald's insurance business had provided well for them over the years. This house, education for the boys, the occasional holiday. If he fell short of the hopes she had had when she married him, at least it wasn't for want of hard work. But Andrew, well, she didn't know what to think. Marrying that black girl and teaching English in the Caribbean village where she grew up. What a waste. A master's degree from a good university and look where he ended up. Not that Mrs. Perkins had anything against the blacks. But what could Andrew and that girl have been thinking? What about children, neither fish nor fowl, belonging to neither group? Mrs. Perkins had seen it before. That friend of Gerald's who married that Jewish girl years ago. Nothing but trouble there.

Mrs. Perkins looked at the clock. Goodness, she'd been sitting and thinking and lost track of the time! She got up and washed her dishes and rinsed out the teapot, then went to her bedroom to change.

The sun on her back was comforting as she toiled in the potting shed. She was pleasantly warm in her cardigan and smock. Repotting her houseplants was an almost daunting task, but she enjoyed it. It was as if she were giving each plant a new home. On his last visit Simon had counted them—the ivies, the hibiscus, African violets, every one of them—and had announced that she cared for thirty-one plants. Why do you need so many? he had asked, sipping his scotch in the living room, his legs crossed, one arm resting languidly on the arm of the sofa. They must be a lot of work. They keep me company, she had replied pointedly. But the remark had been lost on him.

I wonder if he'll remember to call and wish me happy birthday, she reflected once again.

She couldn't remember if he had telephoned last year. These days, bits of her memory were breaking off, crumbling away like loose dirt.

A child's shout drew her attention from the spider plant she was dividing. She tamped down the soil impatiently and walked across the grass to look. The two boys were in her driveway again, bouncing a tennis ball off the side of her house, their shouts echoing in the space between her home and her neighbour's. She had told the boys a dozen times not to play there.

Go away! she demanded. You're damaging the bricks. Go and play in your own driveway.

We're not hurtin' nothin', the older of the two said.

My heavens, Mrs. Perkins muttered, angered by his atrocious grammar as much as his impertinence. When was it that children his age ceased respecting their elders? Not to mention their betters. Look at him. His hands and face are dirty, his hair unkempt, the mud on his arm smeared over that fading bruise.

Why do you insist on coming here? she asked. Play in your own yard.

Mom says we can't, the younger one sniffled, so quietly she could barely hear him.

The two urchins, brothers, belonged to a single mother who lived in the triplex. Mrs. Perkins knew for a fact that she left them alone sometimes, taking off with men who swept into the driveway in flashy cars and honked their horns impatiently. Just yesterday afternoon the woman, in her late twenties—probably had the brats when she was still a teenager, and a good chance it was with two different fathers—was sunning herself in the front yard, lolling on a chaise longue, smoking and sipping from a plastic glass. Drinking up her welfare cheque, no doubt. Flipping through magazines, pausing only to holler at her two boys. A hard-looking character, to be sure.

Still, it wasn't their fault, Mrs. Perkins supposed. Perhaps she shouldn't be so hard on them. She addressed the older boy, who stood holding the ball.

Well, I'd rather you didn't play here. You'll mark the brick with that ball, she repeated. When he didn't reply she added, What happened to your arm? Did you fall?

None of your business, he said in a low voice. His brother giggled.

Mrs. Perkins felt the flush of anger on her neck. Go on, then! she ordered. At once!

The older boy defiantly bounced the tennis ball a few times to make his point, then turned and sauntered off, his brother, wiping a smear of mucus from his upper lip, trailing behind. Mrs. Perkins kept her eye on them until they had crossed the street.

I told you to go play someplace else! she heard behind her back as she returned to her task. The mother, howling like a shrew so the entire neighbourhood knew her business. Honestly!

After she had worked a while longer, Mrs. Perkins sat down on the steps of her back stoop and pulled off her work gloves. Mrs. Perkins cast her eye over her yard, where, within a month, her garden would begin to flourish. Her pride. Still, she never saw the blooms without wishing this place was more like the England of her youth. There, the coming of spring was gentle, like a soft breeze that grew slightly warmer each day. There, you could watch the trees and hedges bud and green, swelling with life. Flowers emerged delicately, their hues gradually changing the appearance of the garden every day.

Here, there was no spring, really. One day snow covered the ground, another it had melted off and the first blush of red on the maples appeared. The new season charged in like a bully into an elevator. The leaves in this country had no subtlety; they burst out overnight, brash and impatient.

Sighing, Mrs. Perkins got slowly to her feet and went inside to prepare lunch.

As she ate her soup and tuna sandwich, her eyes repeatedly rose to the clock on the wall above the sink. One o'clock and still no telephone call from Simon. Her mail lay on the table before her—flyers and bills, not a birthday card in the lot. How inconvenient would it be, she thought, to pick up a card, sign it and drop it in the post?

She put her dishes in the sink and donned her gardening smock, intending to spend the afternoon putting in a few beds of annuals. Some of her perennials were already peeking above the soil. She went outside to find the two boys in her driveway again, this time chalking the outline of a hopscotch game on the asphalt.

Here! You! Stop that! I told you to stay out of my drive. Now go home or I'll call the police!

The boys gathered up their coloured chalk and raced across the street, then turned to stare. The little one stuck out his tongue.

She returned to the yard, grumbling to herself, and knelt at the edge of the grass. To calm herself, she savoured the rich aroma of the damp earth as she turned it with a trowel. After a few minutes, she got up off her knees, walked to the house and propped the kitchen door open. If the telephone rang, she wanted to hear it.

The bedside alarm rang shrilly at five o'clock. Mrs. Perkins always set it when she took her afternoon nap. If she slept too long she would be awake all night. Even as it was, she often had periods of wakefulness. She would read until she felt sleepy again. Part of getting old, she told herself.

She went to the front door, picked up the newspaper from the verandah and carried it through to the kitchen. She tuned the radio to an afternoon phone-in talk show. Today's topic was free daycare. The moderator, an articulate young man who remained refreshingly objective during the show, was explaining how a cabinet minister had floated the idea of subsidized day-care, including no-cost service for the poor.

More handouts, Mrs. Perkins grumbled to herself as she sliced the excess fat from two small pork chops. Everybody has their hand out to the government nowadays. What help did Gerald and I ever get? What's the point of working hard if you get everything for free? Like that woman across the road. Two kids, probably never worked a day in her life. Mrs. Cowan at church last week had opined that some of these young women have kids so they can get the baby bonus or mother's allowance—whatever it's called—and not have to get a job.

Mrs. Perkins glanced at the clock, then poured a tin of mushroom soup over the chops and placed the pan in the oven. She emptied a can of peas into a small pot and put it on the stove, ready to be turned on at the right moment, and began to peel two potatoes. She hoped Simon would call before dinner was ready; it would make her meal so much more pleasant.

But she ate her dinner in front of the television, watching a British drama on the public television network. The British are so much more civilized, she thought. You always say that, Andrew used to taunt her. Ever heard of soccer riots? he would add. Still, she knew she was right.

The movie ended at seven. Mrs. Perkins got wearily to her feet, went into the kitchen and began to wash the supper dishes. I was hungry today, she thought to herself. Two chops and two potatoes! Well, I'm stiff in the mornings and my memory quits on me sometimes, but I still have a healthy appetite. She glanced at the telephone on the wall.

He's not going to call. He's forgotten.

She hung up the tea towel and returned to the living room. She sat in her rocking chair by the window where she would often knit for a while before the nine o'clock news. I'll give him until the news comes on, she decided. Perhaps he's late getting home from work. And yet he always calls as soon as he gets home, she reminded herself, clamping her lips together to stop the quivering of her chin.

Gerald never forgot my birthday, she said out loud as she took up her knitting—a cashmere scarf to match her new spring coat. A bit late, she had told herself when she began it a week ago. Oh well, it will do when autumn comes. No, Gerald always remembered their anniversary, the boys' birthdays, hers. It wasn't too much to ask, surely.

In the corner of her eye she saw the two urchins burst from the side door of the triplex. They scampered up the street in the gathering dusk, slowed to a walk, crossed and ambled along the sidewalk toward her house. They turned into Mrs. Perkins's driveway and out of her line of sight.

That does it, she muttered, dumping her knitting and struggling out of her chair. She threw on her cardigan and pulled open the front door. The boys were sitting close beside one another in the driveway, their backs against her house.

You there! she said. You come with me. We'll solve this once and for all.

The boys reluctantly got to their feet.

What are you gonna do? the older one asked.

Come with me, she repeated.

She marched them across the road and up the driveway to the side door of the triplex. She knocked firmly. No one appeared. Mrs. Perkins rapped again, harder. Behind her, she heard snivelling. The little one, she thought. Presently the door opened.

She was dressed in a tattered flannel house-coat, her hair a tangle, a cigarette dangling from her lip. Mrs. Perkins was almost bowled over by the stench of whisky.

What? the woman demanded. Then, seeing the boys behind Mrs. Perkins, What did they do now? What did you do? she shouted.

Mrs. Perkins drew herself up, aware that the younger boy had tucked in behind her. Such people, she reminded herself, must be dealt with firmly. I've told them several times, she began, to stay out of my driveway. Three times they were there today. Now, I demand that you discipline them or I shall have no choice but to bring in the authorities. Do I make myself clear?

The young woman cursed, reached behind Mrs. Perkins and snatched hold of the younger boy's T-shirt. The two of you get in here! she shrilled. You're nothin' but trouble, both of you. She pushed them ahead of her into the hallway and slammed the door behind her.

My gracious! Mrs. Perkins exclaimed, clutching her cardigan closed as she made her way across the street and onto her verandah to her door. She went inside, locked the door, and resumed her chair and took up her knitting.

But she found it hard to concentrate on her work, and her eyes kept rising to the triplex across the way. The neighbours I'm blessed with! she thought. What's happened to people? They used to be so civil, so polite. She sighed, looked at the clock. It was nine. Time for the news.

I'll wait until nine thirty, Simon, she said out loud. Until the news is over. But no longer.

In her bedroom, moving slowly as if overcome by a lethargy she couldn't explain, she pulled on her nightgown over her head. Sadie, she called. Here, Puss-puss-puss. The cat padded into the bedroom and curled up in her basket. Mrs. Perkins turned on her reading lamp at the side of the bed, set the alarm and pulled back the covers.

The telephone rang.

Happy birthday, Mother!

Simon! Hello, dear! I'm so glad you called.

Of course I called. It's your birthday. Have I ever missed it? How was your day?

No, you've never missed, she thought. How could I have doubted you?

Oh, all right, I suppose, she replied.

You sound a bit tired, Mother. I bet you've overdone the gardening again.

Well, perhaps, just a little. A sudden, unexplained flash of anger. Simon, why did you call so late? I've been waiting—

But it's only seven o'clock, Mother. I got home a bit late today. End of the quarter, lots of accounts to clear up. You know how it is. Mother? Are you there?

Seven o'clock, Mrs. Perkins thought. Of course! I forgot about the time zones! It's only seven o'clock in Vancouver.

Mrs. Perkins plumped her pillow, humming to herself, going over her plans for tomorrow's gardening, looking forward to the day's work. The weather report was promising—mild, with clear skies. She sat down on the bed and kicked off her slippers.

A racing engine and the screech of tires startled her. Another screech, then the slamming of doors. Someone shouted. Such sounds, late at night, terrified her, alone in the house.

She stood and pulled on her housecoat. Furtively, she crept to the living-room window and moved the drape aside, just enough to see out. Two police cars were parked askew on the street, one with its front wheels on the sidewalk, roof lights flashing. An approaching siren wailed, further shattering her nerves. An ambulance swept into the triplex driveway. The doors flew open and two paramedics jumped out, pulled a stretcher from the rear and rushed through the triplex door.

Mrs. Perkins stood rigid, one hand holding her dressing gown closed, the other clenching the drape.

Presently, the paramedics returned. Mrs. Perkins caught sight of a small shape on the stretcher before they hoisted it into the ambulance. The siren whooped again as the vehicle pulled away, its lights blipping against the houses as it roared up the street.

Then two policemen came out of the triplex, holding a third person between them. It was the boys' mother, still in her housecoat. Her head was down, her hands behind her back. The police pushed her into the back seat of the cruiser, slammed the door and drove off.

Moments later, a female officer came out, clutching the younger boy by the wrist, followed by a male officer. The urchin struggled and broke free and dashed down the street. Holding her breath, Mrs. Perkins watched as the male officer gave chase and caught the boy and dragged him kicking back to the remaining cruiser. She saw his profile in the rear window as the car pulled away.

Mrs. Perkins unlocked her front door and stepped outside. She crossed the street. A man emerged from the front door of the triplex, stood in the driveway as if lost. It was the mattress man, in wrinkled trousers, sleeveless undershirt, broken-down bedroom slippers.

I never seen anything like it, he said, his voice quavering, as Mrs. Perkins approached.

What's happened? she asked.

I heard her screamin' all night. You know, on and off, like, he said, lighting a cigarette. His hand trembled as he lowered the cigarette from his mouth. But I never, he went on, I never thought she'd— He shook his head. She threw him down the stairs, he cried. Her own kid. She beat him up and—

Oh my Lord! Mrs. Perkins exclaimed. What an awful thing to do. Is he . . . is he badly hurt?

The man brought his cigarette to his lips again, exhaled the smoke in a thin stream. You hear about these things, he said, as if he hadn't heard her, but you never think—

Well, they won't be hers much longer, Mrs. Perkins pronounced. She'll lose the two of them to Children's Aid. And a good thing—

What do you mean, the *two* of them? the man said. The kid's dead.

apollo and dionysos

"Pathetic," Daniel muttered as he glowered out the Airbus window at a bunch of olive-clad men pushing a wheeled staircase toward the taxiing jet. "The second-biggest city in the country and they don't even have a proper air terminal."

The flight had been a three-and-a-half-hour misery. Inedible food, dry, stale air scraping away at his bronchial tubes, and a plane full of holiday-cheer types revelling at their escape from ice and snow.

"We're here!" his mother announced, running a comb though her hair.

"Finally," his father smiled. Daniel rolled his eyes. Yes, wonderful, he said to himself. Cuba. For two months.

His parents, both doctors, were part of some kind of medical exchange program—Daniel didn't know and couldn't have cared less about the details—and would give talks and study and tour and "network" and do all the other academic things they were so fond of. Daniel, dragged along for his health as well as the "educational experience," had not been allowed to stay home. His acceptance into the university's classical music program had already been granted—two years earlier than normal. Missing forty days of school posed no threat.

The plane lurched to a halt, and the tourists heaved themselves from their seats, jamming the aisle, reaching up to the overhead compartments for their cabin baggage, chattering excitedly about snorkelling, sunbathing, dance classes and Spanish lessons by the pool. Daniel waited until the clogged aisle began to clear, then retrieved his backpack and followed his parents to the door.

A blaze of sunlight, violent in its intensity, greeted him at the top of the stairs. The air was thick with humidity and the odour of vegetation and diesel fuel. Squinting, Daniel walked across the tarmac, baked by the shimmering heat that rose in waves from the ground. Inside the terminal, an air-conditioning duct pumped damp, mouldy air into the room. Daniel could practically feel malignant microbes floating around him. He joined the line for the passport check, his mother's forced good cheer as irritating as the thought of the forty-five-minute bus ride to the resort in Baconao National Park.

The streets of Santiago de Cuba, Daniel observed from the coach window, were narrow and dusty. There were no lawns around the small concrete houses, not much in the way of gardens. In the outskirts, scrawny goats and chickens stood behind makeshift fences of wire, board and cactus. At every intersection, it seemed, men and women and children stood chatting, apparently waiting for rides.

Doesn't anybody in this place have a job? Daniel asked himself.

As the city dropped away behind the bus, the road twisted and turned through the foothills of the Sierra Maestras. Yellow earth, palms, banana trees; steep hillsides, rocky gullies, dry riverbeds; concrete shacks with corrugated iron roofs. Shoeless kids, mangy dogs, women leaning in doorways, looking out at the road.

At last the ocean appeared. Mountains, purpled by haze, seemed to leap into the afternoon sky. With a chirp and a hiss of air brakes, the bus pulled into Club Los Amigos. Three-star rating. Out of a possible five.

Daniel heaved a sigh.

Daniel's room was cramped and sparsely equipped. A small desk, on which his laptop sat open. A TV whose screen was smaller than his computer's; nothing on anyway. The workers had removed one of the single beds and set up a table. It now held Daniel's electronic keyboard; a sheet-music file arranged alphabetically by composer; his books, carefully aligned between two bookends; a stack of DVD movies, laid out in a clear plastic box in the order in which he intended to view them, having planned it so that he could watch one every three days until the ordeal of the trip was over; his CDs—data and music; his asthma puffers.

In his closet he had hung his clothes, grouped by categories: T-shirts, short-sleeved shirts, long-sleeved shirts, trousers. His underwear and handkerchiefs were folded and stowed in drawers. His shoes were neatly arranged on the floor.

He had his own bathroom, with a dripping

tap, a shower stall with a torn plastic curtain, a sink with one glass shelf barely large enough to accommodate his medications and the stack of aromatic non-allergenic soap bars he had brought from home. Each morning someone made his bed, tidied, and shaped his towels into swans.

Daniel's parents were gone most of the day and sometimes evenings. They worked in Santiago, taking a taxi to and fro. Daniel practised in the mornings, read or did logic and math puzzles in his room, occasionally ventured onto the white sand beach, the only person there in long pants, long-sleeved shirt and wide-brimmed hat. His mother warned him each morning about the sun. "You'll burn to a cinder in no time," she predicted, always including a word on the virtues of sunblock.

The resort consisted of a dozen two-storey buildings set around a pool and landscaped grounds with grass, palmettos and bougainvillea hedges tumbling with pink and purple blossoms. The shore was minutes away, offering a bit of shade under trees whose names Daniel could only guess at, assuming he was interested.

The beach bar seemed always to be busy, the speakers hung under the thatched roof booming salsa music. Daniel hated salsa.

The food at the buffet was terrible. Meat and more meat. Rice, with meat. Soup, with meat. Fish. Pasta, with meat sauce. A vegetarian, Daniel would have to subsist on bread and salads and omelettes.

There were only a few people his age at the resort, mostly girls, all giggles and vanity. They strutted around, shoulders back, yearning to be ogled. The guys seemed intent on drinking and smoking as much as they could before they fell over.

As he passed the beach volleyball net on his second day at Los Amigos, he was stopped by a woman's voice. "Hey, man! You play?"

All seven young men and women were tanned and toned, their limbs glowing with oil. Daniel, garbed from head to foot to keep away the sun, muttered, "No, thanks."

"Come on, man, we need a fourth," insisted a sinewy black youth who tossed the ball casually from hand to hand. "Strip down and join us."

One of the other men said something in Spanish, and the women laughed.

"I'm asthmatic. I don't play sports," Daniel said as he trudged through the deep sand. "Besides, I've got better things to do."

As if the Hades in which he was exiled for sixty days was not enough, Daniel found that each time he entered the gallery that led to his room, a blur streaked from beneath a rattan couch, snarling and snapping. A small, terrier-like dog with a patch of bare skin in the centre of its back would stalk him, its ears flat against its head, lips curled to reveal menacing teeth. Heart pounding, Daniel would walk backwards to his door and escape inside.

Daniel alternated between his preference for Mozart ("So serene," he told his father once) and Bach ("So logical"). One morning, he was practising a piano version of Mozart's Adagio from the Clarinet Concerto in A. He wore earphones, but the drone of the air conditioner intruded like a bad smell. He was interrupted by a knock on the door.

"It's me, dear."

Daniel rose and unlocked the door. "What are you doing back so soon?" he asked his mother.

"The hosts at the university have laid on a tour of Santiago for us," she complained. "One of those social obligations. They insisted that you come along. Your father is waiting for us in Céspedes Park, in front of the cathedral."

"I'm not really—"

"You have to go," she cut in. "It would be rude not to. Besides," she added without conviction, "it's a very historic city."

"I'm sure."

"Well, with hundreds of years to work on it, they must have come up with *some*thing interesting," she said.

Four hours later, having suffered the ancient *casa* in Céspedes Park, the cathedral (where Daniel and his parents muttered about superstition and ignorance), three museums, an art gallery, two plazas baking under the afternoon sun, the rum distillery, a factory where men and women sat behind tables rolling cigars while a woman on a stool read stories to them over a loudspeaker—after consuming a number of large bottles of *agua mineral,* Daniel followed his parents and the guide from the university to a graveyard.

The Santa Ifigenia cemetery was, Daniel's father promised, their last stop. Daniel trailed behind his parents and their host, Dr. Mendez, past a pond in the shape of a cross. Narrow sidewalks flanked by flower beds ran between marble graves adorned with statuary angels, crosses and saints and surrounded by wrought-iron fences. The sturdy monuments had been built aboveground. The thought of being literally surrounded by decaying corpses made Daniel wince. In spite of himself, he shuddered as a phrase he had once heard slipped into his mind: city of the dead. But he caught himself. Stupid, he thought. Unreasonable.

"And this way," Dr. Mendez rambled on, "is the tomb of one of our national heroes, José Martí." He led Daniel's parents toward a large octagonal mausoleum.

Daniel hung back. The others were soon out of sight behind the graves. He took a path toward an area where the tombs were less overpowering—simple structures skirted with clean gravel, a few ornamented with baskets of flowers. He found himself by a low iron fence marking the cemetery's border. On the other side, dry brown grass patched the bare ground between thorny shrubs. Cicadas thrummed rhythmically in the hot, still air.

Below the cicadas' song, Daniel heard someone keening tunelessly. He scanned the desolate area beyond the fence. Almost out of sight behind a bush, a figure knelt, her back to him, before a fire of paper trash and twigs. Daniel heard a faint *ching-ching* along with the chanting. The figure moved, tossing something into the flames. *Ching-ching*. She wore a soiled white shirt. Bare soles poked out from beneath a dark skirt.

Her voice was thin and dry. He didn't understand the words, but knew they were not Spanish. The singer poured something onto the fire and the flames brightened. She repeated a single word five or six times, then fell silent.

"More superstition," Daniel muttered. "Stupid nonsense."

The chanter's shoulders stiffened. Her back straightened. She rose slowly and, just as slowly, turned to face Daniel.

She was old, rail thin, her skin like coal. A red bandana covered her head, and brass hoops hung from earlobes that framed a skeletal face, the skin taut over her cheekbones. Copper bracelets adorned skinny wrists. In her claw-like hands she held a leather pouch.

Her piercing black eyes smouldered malevolently. Daniel felt an icy finger jab his spine as she bared her teeth. He took a step back as she reached into the bag—*ching-ching*—and withdrew it, then, with an almost casual flick of her wrist—*ching!*—flung something at him.

Too late, Daniel threw up a hand. Something sharp pinched the soft hollow beneath his Adam's apple. He sucked in his breath. He took a step back, stumbled on the edge of the sidewalk, and fell. He scrambled to his feet. Like a crow, the small dark figure drifted away through the trees, leaving the fire burning. Daniel's hand rose to his throat, felt something hard there, stuck in his skin. He pulled it away, crying out at the burning pain. It looked like a claw, no larger than the end of his little finger. Shreds of fur clung to the base. Disgusted, he threw it aside. He spit on his hands, rubbed them together, dried them on his trousers. He rubbed his throat with his handkerchief. It came away with only a tiny smear of blood.

"Daniel!" His father's voice.

"Coming," Daniel called out. "Be right there!" He trotted back toward the cross-shaped pond and found his parents and their escorts.

"Where were you?" his mother asked, dabbing her damp forehead with a silk scarf.

"I got lost."

"Well, it's time we went back to the hotel. You look pale, dear. The heat must be getting to you."

"Yeah, maybe," Daniel said.

"I'm afraid your father and I have to spend the next three days or so here in Santiago," his mother told him. "Another request to report on our research. We'll be so busy it makes no sense to run back and forth between the city and the hotel."

Daniel nodded absently, looking back over his shoulder.

The next morning, Daniel awoke with a fever scratching at his throat and a throbbing in his temples. By lunchtime his aching bones seemed to have filled with cement. After pulling the drapes across the patio door and turning up the air conditioner, he padded to the bathroom, swallowed some pills and took to his bed. He opened a book but couldn't concentrate. He listened to his CD player, but, after a while, flung it aside. Then he drifted into a hot and sweaty sleep.

In a dream, he lay naked on a cold marble slab, surrounded by gravestones, silhouetted against a full moon. Although he was sick with fear, he had the sense that he belonged there. He heard insects stirring in the grass around the slab and the soft footfalls of larger creatures stalking between the monuments. A dark shape loomed high above him, wavering like a kite, intermittently blocking the moon's cold silver light.

Slowly, implacably, the shape descended, growing larger and gradually acquiring shape. Something familiar came into focus. It was the leathery face of the woman in the graveyard, dark cavities where her eyes should have been. She grimaced, revealing stumpy yellow teeth. She reached out to gather him to her. *Ching-ching.* Cold, bony arms clutched him, tighter and tighter, until his chest was crushed. He gasped and struggled for breath. "No!" he begged. "No!"

Daniel awoke in the grip of a full-scale asthma attack. His lungs seemed collapsed within his aching chest. He crawled, wheezing, to the edge of his bed. Fell to the floor. Pulled himself to his feet. Fumbled in the dark for his puffer. Jammed it in his mouth. Plunged-and-sucked. Sat down, willing himself to fight the instinct to gasp for breath, staring at the crack between the drapes where welcome amber light from the lamps on the grounds seeped through.

After a while, his breathing restored to normal, he went into the bathroom and gulped down half a bottle of water. In the harsh glow of the fluorescent light over the mirror he noticed a tiny scab on his throat in the centre of a patch of angry red skin. It was itchy. Infected, he thought, reaching for his first aid kit.

Daniel kept to his bed for two days, snapping at the maid when she tried to enter, taking no food, only drinking bottled water, fighting off nightmares and the constricting vise of his disease, oscillating wildly between terror and relief.

On the third day, the day his parents were to return, he drifted into wakefulness and got out of bed. It was noon. Standing in the shower, he vigorously rinsed away the sweat and bad dreams. He towelled off, looked in the mirror. The mark on his neck was gone. He grinned at his reflection. "That's better," he said.

Stars sparked in the sky above a calm dark ocean. A powerful animal sprinted along a beach, breathing effortlessly, awash in night odours—the salt sea, fish, the dewy ground that skirted the beach, the blossoms in the hedges. Overhead, Daniel hovered like a kite. He saw the bones and sinews and muscles ripple beneath the creature's skin, felt the heat rising from its back.

The beast was indistinct, a shape only, but Daniel felt its power, its joy as it ran. It swerved inland, crossed a dirt road, slipped into the trees as it headed into the mountains. Daniel soared higher, followed the shape as it disappeared, then reappeared under the trees. Then he veered off, banking like a glider.

Daniel awoke to birdcalls outside his patio door. He stretched languidly, hopped out of bed, drew the curtain aside. Workers with machetes, chatting amiably in Spanish, were cutting the grass between the palmettos and bougainvillea shrubs. The pleasant memory of his dream faded like smoke in a breeze. He showered, took his medications, sauntered out into the morning. At the end of the hall, the little mongrel darted from under the couch and clamped his jaws, snarling, on Daniel's pant leg. He bent over and clouted the mangy animal on its head. The dog released its hold and ran off, yelping. Daniel headed for the dining room. He was hungry.

He spent the day by the pool, under an umbrella, reading and doing crossword puzzles. Occasionally he went to the pool bar and ordered fruit drinks, waiting patiently for his turn as revellers kidded and flirted with each other, trading quips with the bartenders.

For the next few nights, the dream returned. On the fourth night, as Daniel hovered above the loping animal and it veered toward the mountains, he stooped like a hawk, his own indistinct form blending with that of the beast. He was swept away with an exhilaration he had never felt before.

He sat with his parents on the patio, eating breakfast. His father pored over an article in a medical journal as he sipped his coffee. His mother, bored and fidgety when she was away from her work, glanced around the patio and wrinkled her nose as a man three tables away lit up a cigar. She fussed with her napkin.

A new flock of tourists had arrived and the buffet was busy. As Daniel was toying with his toast and jam, a waiter slipped a CD into the stereo beside the drinks cooler, and African rhythms and guitars filled the air. Same table, Daniel mused, same food, same boring tunes.

"Daniel, what on earth has happened to your hands?"

He looked down. Grime discoloured his skin. Dirt was caked under cracked fingernails.

His father looked up from his journal. "Not what you'd call pianist's delicate digits."

His hands, Daniel often thought, were the only part of his body with any strength. A lifetime of piano playing had hardened muscles and tendons. He kept his nails manicured, his skin—except his fingertips where they touched the keys—soft. A pianist, every music teacher he had ever had reminded him, must look after his hands.

But now he was as mystified as his mother.

"Well?" she said.

"Um," he began, wishing that he was a better liar. He knew an I-don't-know wouldn't satisfy his parents. "I fell on the way to breakfast," he said. "There's this ratty little dog, I think it belongs to the maid, and it chases me every morning. And I fell."

His mother pushed a few strands of hair from her damp forehead. The day was already heating up. "Well, be more careful," she advised.

Daniel relaxed. A waitress bent across the table for his plate. Her shirt fell away from her body, revealing the tops of her breasts and a white bra. Daniel diverted his gaze, conscious of her warmth, the odours of her body. He breathed deeply. She straightened up and moved away from the table.

The powerful creature ran, climbing a steep, stony slope to a plateau. The night sky, obscured by clouds, gave no light, but the beast saw easily enough as it sprinted across the dry ground, skirting the small villages, sniffing wood smoke, burned lamp oil, humans, pigs, chickens, horses. In the fields around the tiny settlements, the sharp, heavy odour of goat, the thick scent of cow. Tongue lolling, the beast paced itself, running for the sheer joy of movement, rejoicing in its power and agility, ears tuned to the myriad sounds of the night, eyes afire. When thirsty, it lapped mountain spring water from rocky pools; when hunger pangs creased its stomach, it knew where to find succulent flesh and marrow, and rich, hot blood.

Daniel languished on a chaise longue in the shade of a tree on the beach, watching the waves break on the coral fifty metres from shore. A warm breeze from the water carried the scent of salt and fish. Piano practice had begun to bore him. He no longer read his books or worked on his puzzles; he preferred to soak up the heat and watch and listen.

He heard snatches of conversation whenever he wished, even at a distance. He drew odours from the air at will—the coconut-scented sunblock that the woman walking the shore in front of him had rubbed on her body; beer and rum from the bar; and a hundred different sweats.

He had begun to take some sun, and already a light golden tan tinged his skin. And he no longer felt ashamed to walk bare-chested along the beach. Though he was slender and undeveloped compared to the hard, muscular Cuban men, he glowed with the new power in his limbs. He felt as if he could run for miles, swim across the Caribbean.

The changes had frightened Daniel at first, but now he accepted—welcomed—them without question. The strange occurrences, like the lunchtime he found himself sitting down to a plate of blood-rare roast beef smothered in rich gravy, the breakfast when he tipped his plate to his lips and sucked bacon fat into his mouth, even the morning he rose from the toilet seat and noticed, to his amazement, shreds of fur in his stools—none of these things troubled him now.

Something was happening to him. And he wanted it more than he had ever desired anything.

"Cheers," said his father.

Daniel and his parents clinked glasses. He was allowed wine with dinner that evening, to celebrate. His father had received an award at the conference, and one of his papers was to be published in a medical journal out of Havana.

"It's not exactly *Lancet*," his mother had said when she announced the news, "but it's an honour nevertheless."

They made small talk for a while. Daniel's father commented on Daniel's change in eating habits, apparently pleased. "From vegan to voracious," he said. Daniel didn't tell them he had no need for his puffers any more, or that his medications lay in the bottom of the waste-basket in his room. His mother would worry.

His parents soon fell into shop talk. Daniel made his way to the long buffet table, picking up a new plate. He selected a broiled fish, which had been cooked head and all, and a thick slice of ham. As he turned away, he noticed a young woman serving fresh fruit behind a table in the corner.

Her black skin contrasted sharply with her crisp white smock. As she moved, placing ooz-ing slices of papaya on a platter with a spatula, the supple muscles in her forearms flexed; her long fingers seemed to caress the fruit. Daniel sucked in the rich scents—pineapple, mango, banana and the thick cream in the bowl at the end of the table; the woman's hair, the per-fume that floated like a cloud above the layer of perspiration. She had wide eyes, slightly slanted, and thick wiry hair drawn back from her face and held behind her head with a sim-ple copper ring that glowed when she moved her head.

Daniel returned to his table. He cut his ham into chunks and pushed them into his mouth, gulping them down, his eyes directed across the room to the woman behind the fruit stand.

"What are you staring at?" his mother demanded.

His father pointed with his chin. "I think it's that girl over there."

As his parents looked toward the fruit stand, Daniel cut the head off his fish and popped it into his mouth, chomping noisily.

"Daniel, you really must stop this ogling," his mother said, turning back to the table. "It's rude and demeaning. You above all people should know women aren't objects. You were raised better."

Behind his mother's head, Daniel saw the woman look his way. She fixed him with her eyes, her face expressionless.

She knows, he thought.

Later, lying in bed, Daniel easily directed his hearing to the next room, where his parents went through their preparations for bed.

"Did you notice your son at dinner? You need to talk to him about his staring. He's stripping them naked with his eyes. It's embarrassing."

"Oh, leave him alone. He's finally—at his age!—showing an interest in females and you're upset about it. Well, I'm not. Frankly, I was beginning to wonder about him."

"Oh for heaven's sake! Just because he hasn't fallen for the whole do-it-if-it-feels-good ethic these days. I don't want him to become a boor."

Daniel awakened early with the familiar comfortable ache and languor in his limbs. Standing at the sink, he scrubbed his hands with a brush, scouring the dirt from beneath his nails and the creases in the skin around his knuckles. He showered and brushed his teeth, barely noting that one of his upper canines was chipped, combed his hair, removing a burr, and put on a pair of shorts and a tight T-shirt.

He listened outside his parents' room, heard his father's snore and his mother's deep breathing, and headed to breakfast without them. As he passed, the little terrier cowered under its couch, ears flat to its head, whining.

In the dining room, Daniel asked the man making the omelettes for three raw eggs. The man shrugged, cracked the eggs into a cup and put it on Daniel's tray. Daniel selected half a dozen pork sausages, spooning grease onto his plate, and took a piece of toast. Alone at his table, he poured the eggs down his throat, washed them down with hot black coffee, then made a sandwich of sausages slathered with ketchup and melted fat.

Afterwards, he strolled into the lobby shop and bought a bathing suit. In his room, he donned the new trunks, oiled his body with sunblock, then headed for the beach. He took a swim, reapplied sunblock and walked the length of the beach, gathering snatches of conversation and eddies of smells, squeezing wet sand between his toes, revelling in the hot caress of sun on his skin. He retraced his steps to the beach bar. He ordered a beer and stood sipping it, watching the volleyball game.

She was there, among eight shouting and laughing players, a mix of tourists and hotel staff. One of the tourists, a heavy, well-built man in his twenties, crowed whenever his team scored a point.

At length, a Cuban dropped out, picking up a tank top from a chair nearby and heading toward the main building. The game ceased. Heads swivelled.

"What about him?" someone said. Eyes focused on Daniel.

"Why not?" the muscular guy jeered, addressing the shorthanded team. "It's not like you'll catch up to us anyway. Not with him on your side."

Daniel stared at the man. "I'll play," he said.

Daniel knew the rules, knew how to play from lessons at school, classes he had attended only under duress. To his surprise, he held his own, fumbling a few balls at first, then improving rapidly. What he lacked in experience he made up for with speed and agility. Soon he was at the net, and his team had caught up.

He watched intently as the young woman from the dining-room fruit stand prepared to serve. She wore a banana yellow bikini. Daniel took in her smells, noted the muscles rippling beneath the skin of her thighs, the sheen of sweat across the tops of her breasts. She served overhand. Behind him, his teammates set up the ball. Daniel jumped, timing his spike perfectly. His hand was far above the net when he drove the ball downward. It slammed—*Thwack!*— into the chest of the man who had mocked him.

His arms windmilling, the man stumbled backwards and sat down heavily, grunting.

Cheers from behind Daniel. The man shook his head, fixed Daniel with a murderous look as his face turned crimson. He leaped to his feet and rushed across the sand, ducking under the net.

"I'll teach you to—"

Daniel sidestepped the rush and spun the man around, tripping him. As the man crashed to the sand, Daniel dropped one knee to the man's chest and gripped his throat with one hand. He snarled, baring his teeth, squeezing his fingers tighter, his tendons contracting like piano wire, oblivious to the choking and splutters coming from the man's open mouth.

"Let him go!" someone yelled. "He's choking him," came another voice. Arms pulled him backwards. He looked up. She was watching him, wide-eyed, her mouth open, a string of spittle joining her lips. She licked it away, closed her mouth, the intimation of a smile crossing her lips.

Daniel allowed himself to be pulled to his feet. He brushed sand from his knees, then walked away.

That afternoon, he sat at his keyboard, earphones clamped to his head so that only he could hear. He played by ear, music he normally refused even to acknowledge. He surrendered to the passion of Liszt, alternately pounding and caressing the keys. After a while, he played impromptu, creating as he went, his torso rising and dipping, his head bobbing, sweat dripping from his brow. He played and played, insanely, with no control but that imposed by the music, until he fell from his chair, exhausted.

The beach party, to be held on Daniel's last night in Cuba, had been the talk of the resort for a week. Daniel had joined his parents in their derision, pretending all the while. The hypnotic rhythm of drums could be heard as the three family members strolled through the grounds to their rooms after dinner. Daniel waited, fidgeting, drumming his fingers, until he heard the deep breathing of sleep through the wall. Then he dressed and left his room.

Tables and chairs had been set up in the sand. A bonfire crackled, and the bar was crowded and raucous. A large number of resort guests had turned up, along with a few workers. Daniel joined the crush at the bar, his eyes scanning the beach. He drank his first beer quickly and ordered another, carrying it to the edge of the water. He stood ankle deep in the lapping waves, facing the shore. Finally he caught sight of her. She was dancing with one of the young men who regularly played volleyball.

The tune ended and another began, with a faster beat that seemed to reach out and clutch him at the centre. The young woman left her partner and approached Daniel. She wore a white dress with full skirt and a scoop neck. She was barefoot, and copper bracelets adorned her wrists. She took Daniel's hand and led him to the patch of sand where the dancing was taking place. They said nothing to one another. Daniel watched her feet, immediately picked up the simple steps, and gave himself up to the sounds.

The surf pounded, an arhythmic backdrop for the narcotic, complex cadence of the drums. The music seeped down into him, slaking a need in him, the way spring water is absorbed by dry, porous rock. The woman danced with the grace of a cat, the intensity of a storm. The drumbeats welded the two of them together as their feet pounded the sand, their eyes fixed on each other. Daniel heard only the surf and the drums and her breathing, felt only her heat.

The dance had ended late, and the full moon was rising. Daniel paced his room, unable, despite his fatigue, to stop moving. He stripped off his damp clothing, showered, dressed in dry trousers and T-shirt. On his dresser top, his suitcases sat open. In one, clothes and shoes in a jumble; in the other, a chaos of CDs, DVDs, books and sheet music. Departure time was seven a.m.

He heard something outside. He shut off the air conditioner, slid open the patio door. A gecko scurried across the stones. Daniel was keenly aware of crickets, insects creeping in the grass, the soft clatter of palmetto fronds in the night breeze. And something else. The quiet footfalls of an animal, padding restlessly back and forth behind the resort.

A soft growl.

Daniel felt his heart accelerate, his breathing become shallow and rapid. He backed into his room, then strode to the patio, returned to the room, downed a glass of water in the bathroom, stalked to the patio door once more. He directed his attention to his parents' room, the sounds of their sleeping. He glanced at his computer, his keyboard, his books, the airplane ticket at the edge of his desk. He heard another growl, more distant this time, then sensed rather than heard the footfalls recede.

Daniel looked into his room once more, then stepped across the threshold. The waving palmetto fronds scattered splinters of moonlight across the patio. Daniel made for the beach. He strode past the empty bar, the tables and upended chairs, far down the strand, where waves crashing against the reef hurled streaks of spume into the air. Piece by piece, he flung his clothing away until he was naked. He lay down on the damp sand, waiting for sleep.

AUTHOR'S NOTE

In Greek mythology, the god Apollo is associated with music, poetry, harmony and reason. We find his spirit also in mathematics and classical architecture. He favours reason and balance.

Dionysos is sometimes referred to as "the party god," but that's too simplistic. He represents the passions, energy, creativity and sexuality. If Apollo is classical, Dionysos is with the Romantics.

It is sometimes said that the human personality contains both gods, and we are happiest when there is a balance between their spirits.

window tree

"Your head so much concerned with outer,
Mine with inner, weather."
—ROBERT FROST

This place beside the window has been my favourite for as long as I can remember. The stuffed chair with the flower print and matching ottoman, the table with the brass lamp and telephone. From here I can look out over the yard all the way to the river.

The maple that shades the back of the house was already old when Mother and Father bought the property and began to build, the same year I came into the world. Father always joked that he planted it for me, but even early on I knew he couldn't have. I call it my window tree. I've watched it change with the seasons, and I know its every stage, from the moment the frost leaves the ground in May until November winds send the sap to the roots.

In the morning sun, every leaf is a green lamp. At dusk, its shadow embraces the house. In winter, the branches click and clatter in the wind that sweeps off the river, and summer breezes set the leaves rustling in quiet conversation.

"Tree at my window, window tree." It was the first poem he taught us. By Robert Frost, America's greatest poet, he announced that first day in October after Mrs. Smart had fallen ill and we had suffered an endless stream of supply teachers for two weeks, accomplishing nothing and learning less. Then he came, with his thick leather-bound complete poems of Frost under his arm, walking into the classroom that Wednesday morning as if he had been our teacher for years, as if he owned the school.

Not conceited. How we hate conceit! No, more like a quiet confidence, a clear sense of purpose and direction that carried us along. The class clowns shut up quickly and joined in. After a couple of days' grace, a few of the guys tried him on for size, asking barbed questions, giving cynical answers to his questions. But he outwitted them every time, and won most of them over with his jokes. He had a mind like a razor, but there was never an edge to his humour, not a hint of sarcasm, not like a couple of teachers I could name, who got their kicks by putting kids down.

Most of the girls didn't agree with me that he was cute, with curly black hair, an aquiline, almost noble nose and a certain look that played at the corners of his eyes when he was kidding. He wasn't big or hard or strong—the opposite, a dancer rather than a football player, and a few inches taller than I. You could tell by the way he read poetry or lines from *Hamlet* that he had what every boy I had ever met lacked—empathy. You knew he would understand you. And he could be sensitive without being feminine. Most of all, he wasn't afraid to show emotions, or respond to them.

After a week with him, I didn't care if Mrs. Smart ever came back, and I wasn't alone.

On the first essay I wrote for him—on "The Road Not Taken"—I worked even harder than I usually do. He made you want to do your best; somehow you felt you'd be disappointing him if you didn't. In my interpretation I wrote that I often feel like the speaker in the poem. I usually find myself at odds with other kids. I don't find it hard to resist peer pressure and usually make my own decisions. Result? I'm sometimes branded a snob or a loner. Like the poem says, I choose the road that hasn't had much wear. Anyway, I didn't expect anything more than my usual C+ or B. He gave me an A–.

On the day he handed the essays back, he told the class he wanted to interview each of us and go over our papers. He set us to reading ahead in *Hamlet* and called people up to his desk, one by one, in alphabetical order. Those he didn't get to in class, he said, had to come in after school. I sat through the period, pretending to read, hoping my name, Woodside, wasn't called. He got as far as U before the bell rang. That left Todd Urquhart and me.

At the end of the day I left most of my books in my locker, then pushed through the throng in the halls to the washroom, where I combed my hair and dabbed a bit of cologne at my throat. When I got to the English classroom, Todd was already there. He was a shapeless lump whose clothes never seemed to fit, always with a bewildered look on his face that made him appear kind of innocent. He sat in a chair beside the teacher, hunched over, concentrating on whatever was being said.

Afternoon sun, woven into irregular shapes by the big sycamore outside the window, dappled the desks and rear wall, with its posters of literary figures and grammar tips. The room was warm and quiet, the murmuring of voices at the front of the room like a gentle breeze.

I took a seat at the back, opened my book and began work on a math problem. My stomach felt like it had a knot in it, pulled tighter with each moment that passed. I couldn't help looking up every few minutes toward his desk. I tried the problem three times and came up with three different answers, each one more wrong than the last. Finally, a chair scraped the floor and Todd heaved himself to his feet. He shambled to the door, rolling his essay into a tube as he went, and left the room.

Okay, Shawna, you're next, he said.

I walked to his desk, placed my essay before him and sat down in the chair beside him. He had loosened his tie and rolled his shirt sleeves to his elbows, and the sunlight highlighted the black hairs on his slender forearms. I noticed for the first time how pale his eyes were, almost translucent, and I could smell, beneath the odour of chalk, the remnants of aftershave.

He began to discuss my writing and my interpretation of the poem. He had a way of making every comment sound like a compliment. Even the weaknesses in my style or analysis were described in positive terms. And as he talked, pointing out areas that could be improved— sentence structure, a thought awkwardly expressed—I began to wonder how, with all its faults, my essay had earned an A–. If it had been Mrs. Smart talking—not that she would have; she never interviewed us to discuss our work—she would have simply flagged each weakness with a red X and deducted half a mark.

I wanted to ask him, but lost my courage. He was so earnest, so sincere when he offered a suggestion, smiling each time. Once he patted my hand where it rested on the edge of his desk. He was in no hurry to finish. And it became clear to me after a while that he was enjoying our conversation as much as I was, and the tension drained from my neck and shoulders as I focused my eyes on the dust motes floating in the bar of sunlight that slanted across the corner of his desk.

He began to talk past the essay, asking about my interests—clubs, teams, hobbies—and I replied that I wasn't a joiner.

Ah, a loner. He smiled. As you said in your analysis of the poem. I'm a bit that way myself, he added. He sat back in his chair, one arm hung languidly over the back, and his shirt parted below the knot in his tie where one button had come undone, revealing the fine, curled hair on his chest. Then he shifted his weight and the tie fell into place, covering the opening.

Well, he said, I guess I'll see you tomorrow.

Slowly, I gathered my things and made my way to the door, closing it softly behind me.

Out in the hall, a group of boys stood before open locker doors, books and gym bags scattered at their feet. Sharp banter, jokes and insults, shot from mouth to mouth like missiles. They began to kick something back and forth, laughing, jeering at one of their number, a kid I recognized but didn't know.

Knock it off, he yelled to one, then the other. Knock it off!

Somebody kicked the object in my direction. A cheer burst out as it landed at my feet. I shoved it away with the toe of my shoe. It was a jockstrap, soiled and limp. I turned away and headed down the hall as, behind me, laughter rose like a cloud of starlings.

Could they possibly realize, I wondered, how infantile they were? How boring in their pathetic attempt at cleverness? I might have expected crass behaviour like that from niners, but I knew a couple of the group. They were in my grade. In a little less than a year, they'd graduate.

I thought of the only boys I had ever dated. Marty Jersperson, who took me to a party and had to get himself sodden with beer before he worked up the courage to feel me up. When I pushed him away his face flooded with amazement. Dirk Balderson, who begged me to help him write a book report on *The Diviners*. I'm no good at that stuff, he told me. I wondered out loud if he had liked the book. Are you kidding? came the sneering reply. What do I care about some whining woman and her problems? Then why had he chosen it? There's *Notes* on it. You can get them at the bookstore, he said. Sam Kogawa was different, and not because he was Asian. He was more mature. But all he wanted in life, he told me more than once, was to make money.

I ambled home from school the afternoon I got my essay back, kicking fallen leaves out of my path. There was a chill in the air, like a keen new edge. I found I couldn't keep the new teacher out of my mind.

Throughout the autumn and into the deepening winter, I dreaded the return of Mrs. Smart. Guiltily, I hoped that whatever illness she had— rumours claimed everything from appendicitis to liver trouble to brain cancer—would not be cured. And finally, early in the new year, he broke the suspense. He stood at the front of the room, his face expressionless, and told us we would be stuck with him for the rest of the school year, then grinned his boyish grin.

A few of the guys cheered. Mrs. Smart, he went on, had had an operation on her heart, a successful procedure. But she would need months to convalesce. Tell her to take all the time she wants, one of the guys quipped. I caught his eye and smiled at him, but he looked away and picked up a piece of chalk from the ledge under the blackboard. I understood. He couldn't show his feelings for me, not in front of the others.

With each day that passed, the bond between us grew. I made excuses to come to

his—our—room after school. Not every day—
that would have spawned whispers—but a few
times a week. I would always prepare a question
ahead of time, about the day's lesson or the
homework assignment, so anyone who saw us
would think I was getting extra help. During
these meetings he was always professional, even
proper, but in his jokes, in the way he answered
my questions or offered advice, there was a sort
of undercurrent, an unspoken extra, that reas-
sured me, and spoke louder than his words.

And when I wasn't with him or near him,
while I walked to and from school, when I
whiled away the hours in this chair, gazing
across the yard to the river, I called him into my
mind. I went over his every word to me that
day, reassuring myself that my perceptions were
correct, savouring every moment I had spent
with him.

And I began to look to the future. We could
never be together during the school year, but
summer would bring sixty days of freedom for us.
I imagined a cabin or resort at the edge of a lake,
far away, where no one knew either one of us,
where we could be ourselves, together, and
express our love for each other openly. We could
take long walks in the summer heat, sail, swim.

And in our cabin at night we would be as isolated and free as if we inhabited a fortified castle. Silly, romantic pipe dreams, I told myself. But still.

When June finally rolled around, I began to formulate a plan. Until then I had resisted the urge to call him—sometimes with such difficulty that I found myself with the phone in my hand. I knew he wanted to hear from me, but we couldn't be too careful. Any hint of our relationship would get him into serious, even criminal, trouble. I constantly reminded myself, as the snows receded with glacial slowness and the days grew longer, of the Guestier case. He was a teacher at the other high school in town. He lost his job and teaching licence over a girl in his graduating class. It was in the papers for months. He had claimed the girl was lying, but it didn't matter.

I chose the afternoon of my final exam, a symbolic day in more ways than one. I rushed through the questions, unable to give them my full attention. Once I walked out of the school, the summer was mine. But it was more than that. It was the end of my high-school years, the beginning of my adult life, and I would be free of the suffocating conventions of my teens. That night, in this chair, with my stomach fluttering and my hand shaking, I keyed his telephone number into the handset.

He answered on the first ring, as if he had been waiting by the phone. He seemed distant, a little shy, even, just as I felt. I began by telling him how much I had enjoyed his course, and apologized for the immaturity shown by some of the other kids. He replied that I had made great progress, that he had enjoyed teaching me, that he had appreciated our talks. When I asked about his plans for the summer, he faltered. Nervous, I thought. This is all new to him. It must seem strange, beginning a relationship with a student—the age difference, the problems that would come up. So I eased the way for him. I asked when we should get together and talk about the summer. Still a little awkward, he suggested we should talk at the prom. Then, more confidently, yes, he repeated, we have to talk, and the prom is the best place.

I hadn't planned on going. But since he had all but invited me to be his date—he couldn't put it that way, couldn't come right out with it, not under the circumstances—well, I told myself, I'd better go!

I don't know, because I'd never been to one, but they say the hardest part about the whole prom evening is picking out a dress. That's almost right. I had a horrible time finding something mature enough. But, finally, I settled on organdy in pale blue with spaghetti straps. More difficult than the search for a dress was explaining to Father and Mother that I was going alone. You never go to dances, Mother pointed out with her usual tact. I never get asked, I wanted to say. Whoever heard of going stag to a prom? Father asked a dozen times, and he actually used the word *stag*. Times have changed, I told them. Lots of kids, both sexes, go single—and they have a great time. You don't need to have a date, I explained, thrilled by the secret knowledge that, really, I *did* have a date.

Prom night came, a perfect evening—mild, with a light breeze heavy with the fragrance of blossoms, an almost-full moon. I took a taxi to the school, smirking inwardly at the pretentious classmates who arrived—a few already drunk—in white limousines. I got there about forty-five minutes into the dance, and the gym, pulsing with music, hung with bunting, was packed with bodies gyrating in the semi-dark under a huge revolving glitter ball. An arch at the main door into the gym was festooned with pink paper roses. Inside, a long, linen-covered table held half a dozen punch bowls and stacks of paper cups.

I clutched my evening bag, fingers picking at the decorative pearls stitched to the outside, and watched the dancers. Around me, my twittering classmates pretended to absolutely *love* each other's dresses. I greeted a few, engaged in some short conversations, my eyes on the dance floor.

I didn't see him. I crossed under the arch again, strolled around the halls, stepped outside to the parking lot where a few guys were smoking cigarettes or drinking from the trunks of cars. The night air was soft and the breeze had dropped. Music pulsed from the gym and occasionally a cynical laugh from one of the boys scissored the mood.

I went back inside and sipped a cup of punch. It was awful, sickly sweet with cherry and peach. Terry Savitch asked me to dance and I accepted. It was a slow tune, but Terry behaved himself, made me laugh a few times as he told me about his part-time job at our local big-box hardware store.

And then, just as the tune ended, I saw him. He wore a tux, with a carnation at the lapel, his hair slightly mussed from dancing. I imagined that even from this distance I could see the smile at the corner of his pale eyes. He was leaving the dance floor. And he had with him a woman I didn't recognize.

I stood gaping, hardly noticed when Terry said something. She wasn't a teacher at our school, that much I knew. She was taller than he was, almost radiant in a rose-coloured, scoop-necked gown, her blond hair swept up. She walked with the kind of casual elegance I had envied all my life, her hand on his shoulder as he led her toward the arch.

I pushed my way toward them, his telephone statement that we should talk tonight uppermost in my mind. Perhaps she taught at the other school, I thought as I followed them out of the gym, my eyes on his shoulders. She was chaperone for her students. Or a relative. Maybe he was being cautious, covering himself so that when he danced with me, which he would want to do more than once, people wouldn't wonder, wouldn't take notice and gossip.

The pair moved quickly along the hall to the outside door. I almost called his name, but checked myself, not wanting to attract attention.

They ambled across the parking lot, past the boys, who tossed away their cigarettes and tried to look innocent. I veered off, circled around the lot along the edge of the football field. I caught sight of them again standing beside a small sports car. It wasn't his. I stood just under the bleachers, beyond the faint light from the parking lot.

She's leaving, I thought. He's seeing her off and then he'll come back into the school and look for me. I'd better go, I decided, so I'll be inside when he returns. And right then, the woman put her arms around his neck. She kissed him as his arms encircled her waist. It was not a kiss between friends. He bent her back slightly, one hand caressing her bottom.

A cramp seized my abdomen, staggering me, and I leaned against the bleachers. My breath came in gasps, my knees threatening to give. I fell to my hands and knees, saw chewing gum wrappers, fast-food boxes, cigarette butts, and vomited onto the dewy ground.

I love this place. The window is open, and the odour of fresh-cut grass slips across the sill and into my room, like a secret. The leaves on the window tree are full and broad, deep, waxy green on the weather side, pale and delicate underneath. This chair is like an embrace. Hot chocolate in my favourite cup on the table beside the phone sends up a tendril of steam that bends in the breeze from the window.

Regret is a stone in my chest, regret for what has to be done. He can't be allowed to prey on other girls, to dupe them as he did me. Until today I couldn't bring myself to act. No, until my report card came in the mail and I saw the C beside "English," I was unable to admit to myself the depth of his betrayal.

It will be hard. The police will ask a lot of questions. Mother and Father will be upset, angry because their daughter was taken advantage of. The case might even reach the papers. If it does, I'll hold my head up. The days when women felt guilty are long since gone. Besides, I have an obligation to others. And I'll do my duty.

I have to.

chumley

I tem one in the "Just when you thought things couldn't get any worse" department: first day, second semester. Wet snow, blustery winds, the streets and sidewalks skirted with grimy slush. Half past eight in the morning. I reported as ordered (as threatened) to the principal's office, stood on the blue carpet in front of his desk as he tapped computer keys, making me wait to show me how unimportant I was.

"How many hours left, Vic?" he asked, finally looking up.

"Um, two, sir."

"Nice try. It's five."

One day last semester, during lunch period, a couple of retards in the graduating class tried to paint a design on the chest of my new rugby shirt by squirting mustard and ketchup from plastic dispenser bottles. As soon as they started in, I dropped my plate of fries and shoved the nearest one into the condiments table. As if they had rehearsed it, they flung their bottles aside and started pounding on me.

The school has a zero-tolerance policy on fighting. The two goons got a week's suspension; I got thirty hours' "community service"— slaving for the principal. He told me he had let me off easy because I had been attacked first (assault with a deadly condiment). I would have preferred the suspension. Following his neatly typed list of instructions, I spent my lunch periods and an hour after school each day cleaning up the caf, shovelling snow from the sidewalks and wrestling huge recycling bins full of cans and bottles to the collection area behind the school. By the time the semester had ended, I had served most of my sentence.

The principal said, "I have an assignment for you. A little bit of time each day until the end of the week. Then you're a free man again."

"I can hardly wait to get started," I said.

His lips parted slightly to reveal an even

row of off-white teeth, but the rest of his face was like a plastic mask.

"We have a new student," he said. "He's in your grade. You are to show him the ropes. Make sure he finds all his classrooms, the cafeteria and so on. Try not to sour him on the teachers you don't happen to like."

"So I shouldn't mention math class," I interrupted, but he rolled on.

"At the end of each day you will escort him to his bus stop. On Friday afternoon, he will report to me and tell me how helpful you've been. You *will* be helpful, won't you, Vic?"

"I wouldn't have it any other way."

"He'll meet you by the head secretary's desk at 8:45."

The fact that the principal wanted me to show a new kid around didn't mean the kid was stupid. Our school was more than a century old and it had so many wings and additions stuck onto it that, until you'd spent a week or two, you needed a map to get from place to place.

"What's his name?" I asked.

"He'll introduce himself," the principal replied, giving me the same tight-lipped smile.

"He's a little . . . unusual. So you two should get on well together."

"What do you mean, 'unusual'?"

"Have a nice day, Vic."

I stood at the entrance to the main office. Students streamed in the front doors, unzipping coats, shrugging off backpacks, jostling and calling out to one another, taking places in the alphabetically organized lines for their new timetables. Then I spotted him.

He strode into the school, a scuffed briefcase in one hand and a cane (that's right, a cane) in the other. On his head, a checkered cap with a bill at the back as well as the front, with little ear flaps tied over the crown with ribbons. A long trench coat belted at the waist and buttoned to his Adam's apple. And around his ankles, almost covering shiny black leather shoes, some kind of cloth wrapping. With buttons. He looked like an escapee from an old black-and-white movie on TV.

My first thought was that he must be crazy. He was *asking* for ridicule in a get-up like that. The kids would tear him to shreds before he got two steps down the hall.

He looked around calmly, then put down his briefcase and sat on one of the benches near the door. Twisting the cane between his hands, he broke it down into three pieces and put them in the briefcase. He bent, unbuttoned the anklet things, folded them and dropped them in after the cane. Next, the goofy hat. He stood, picked up the briefcase and, releasing the top button of his coat as he walked, headed toward me.

Bounced would be a better word. As if he didn't look nutty enough, he walked funny, shooting upwards with each step as if he had springs under the balls of his feet. He marched straight down the hall in this piston-like manner and stopped.

"Excuse me. Are you, by any chance, Victor Kendall?"

I was expecting a reedy drone, but his voice was strong and confident.

And his accent was British. *Really* British.

"Vic," I corrected him.

"How do you do. Allow me to introduce myself. I am Chumley N. Hyde-Barrington."

He held out his hand and we shook like insurance salesmen.

"N.?" I said.

"For Nigel, I'm afraid. After my maternal grandfather. I understand you've been assigned to assist me," he said.

Every word that came out of his mouth made him sound as if he thought he was better than you. As if he was looking down on you.

"Yeah, well, don't get used to it," I answered, thinking, I'm stuck with this weirdo for a week. "Let's get our timetables, then I'll show you around."

He stood behind me in line and I pretended he wasn't there. Everybody around him did exaggerated double takes, or stared, or just smirked and laughed. A few dropped prickly comments in stage whispers. He stood like a post, eyes forward, as if he was alone on a deserted beach.

I knew the gods were against me when I read our timetables. Not only had we been assigned lockers side by side, we shared two classes, math and English—probably the principal's idea of a joke. With the new kid bouncing along behind me like an aristocratic kangaroo, I showed him his classrooms and then took him to the lockers.

He removed his trench coat and put it inside. He was wearing a sports jacket, a white shirt and an ascot. (That's right, an ascot.) He snapped the lock shut, picked up his briefcase and looked at me expectantly.

"The last thing I need to show you is the caf," I said. "Then you can be on your way."

The caf was a zoo, jammed with students milling around, waiting for first class to start. Maddie and Phil were at our usual table. Phil had a solitaire hand laid out and Maddie sat beside him, offering advice, as usual.

"Hey, guys," I said. I pointed over my shoulder with my thumb. "Meet Chumley Nigel Hyde-Barrington the Fourth."

Maddie's big blue eyes widened and her jaw dropped. Phil, always cool, merely allowed his eyebrows to rise a little. The new kid stepped forward like a soldier volunteering for a difficult mission and put out his hand.

"How do you do."

From his seat, Phil shook with him. Maddie struggled for control, her face pink, her lips pressed together as she bit back a laugh. She extended her hand like a queen.

"Charmed, I'm sure," she squeaked.

Maddie wasn't ordinarily a squeaker. She was a stocky (she'd cut out my liver if she heard me use that word) reddish blonde who always seemed as if she'd forgotten to take her hyperactivity medication. Most of all, she was LOUD, as if she spoke in capital letters.

"What kind of name is Chumpey, anyway?" Phil asked, getting the name wrong on purpose, I was sure.

"It's Chumley, my dear chap. British, actually. And Victor is making a jest at my expense, I'm afraid. I am not, nor have I ever been, 'the Fourth.'"

Then he kissed Maddie's hand before sliding onto the bench across from her. I sat down beside him.

"Are you like this ALL the time?" Maddie demanded.

"I beg your pardon?"

Phil smirked and tossed me a look that said, This should be fun.

"Can you BELIEVE this guy?" Maddie elbowed Phil and put on a phony (and bad) English accent. "I say. PIP PIP. I BEG your pardon, OLD BEAN."

I looked at CN, as I had already begun to think of him. There wasn't a trace of anger on his face. He even smiled.

"People in glass houses," he said.

"HUH? WHAT did he say?" Maddie appealed to me. But Phil cut in.

"Bad news on the academic front, Vic. Maddie and I both have Quinn for math again."

"So do we," I said.

"Oh, GOOD," Maddie drawled, rolling her eyes. "We can all be TOGETHER."

I dragged CN around like an anchor for the rest of the day, pointing out as much as I could and giving him as little advice as possible. He asked no questions. When classes were finished he retrieved his old-spy-movie coat from his locker, put his cane together, pulled his cap tightly onto his head as if he was afraid a sudden wind would come along and buttoned up his anklets.

"What are those things, anyway, and why do you wear them?" I asked.

He looked up and smiled. "My dear chap—"

"Listen, man. Get this straight. I'm not *yours,* I'm not a *chap,* whatever that is, and if you keep saying *dear* to people of your own gender someone around here is going to put you on the floor."

Way to go, Vic. I thought. No way this loser is going to give you a good report now. I waited for his reaction. He slowly buttoned the second anklet, stood, belted his trench coat—and laughed.

"Fair enough, Victor—Vic. These items of apparel are called spats. Useful for keeping the footwear unsoiled. A trifle out of date, one knows. But I rather fancy them. So there it is."

There *what* is? I wanted to ask, but instead I muttered, "Let's go," and led him out of the school to the bus stop. He knew where it was, but the principal had said to escort him there.

"This is it," I said, then added uselessly, "your bus stop."

"Ah, yes," he said, looking the pole up and down as if he'd never seen one before.

"Um . . . Look, er, Chumley. You know where everything is now, right? The caf, your classes, the whole thing."

He nodded.

"See, the thing is," I went on hopefully, "you won't really need me the rest of the week, will you?"

"Dreadfully sorry, old—ah, sport," he said. "Know I must be a terrible bore. But I'm afraid you're stuck with me until Friday at, ah—" he looked at his watch, a cheap discount store version, "at four on the clock. That was the bargain, if I'm not mistaken."

Bargain, my butt, I thought. In a bargain both sides get something out of it.

"Perfect," I said, turning away.

CN was the biggest pain in the rear end that I'd ever met in my life. Everything about him, his stupid clothes, his snotty accent, the impression he gave that he could walk on water, that you weren't fit to wash his undies—all that, along with his weakness, filled me with scorn and contempt. I made it through that first week, barely, without killing him, then brushed him off.

But I shared two classes with him. So, without really wanting to, I watched him from a distance. The teachers didn't know what to make of him. They treated him carefully, as if at any moment he might fall down foaming at the mouth. He was always polite, but you could see they didn't trust his good manners, sensing mockery just under the surface.

The kids kept up the attacks—ridicule and sneers and half-concealed giggles from the girls, not-so-gentle jostling and name-calling from the guys. CN let it all bounce off. And what amazed, confused and sometimes enraged me—he took it with his chin up. No trading insult for insult, no hurt looks, no revenge. You'd have thought he was in the middle of some invisible force field that nothing could get through.

To be insulted and humiliated like that and not respond—how, I asked myself, could he put up with it? What a jerk, a weakling, a coward.

It was Maddie who came around first. She saw Chumley, at first, as a pathetic loser, then, gradually, as a creature who needed to be mothered. "He's not THAT bad," she admitted one day when I was ragging on about him, and I knew that her heart had gone soft. CN's fair good looks didn't hurt. Maddie began to get that glint in her eye—Phil called it the fox-in-the-henhouse stare—whenever CN was near.

Phil caved in next. "He's okay, I guess." Which, from Phil, was the ultimate stamp of approval. One day he even asked CN for his help with a math problem. And he got the help, with no strings or conditions, no You-wouldn't-talk-to-me-for-a-month-and-now–you-want-my-help? guilt trip from CN. "Certainly, old sport. Delighted," was all he said.

And me? I didn't join the chorus of approval. One afternoon when CN had put up with another snarky comment from a girl named Liz, just as he was closing his locker door beside me, I said under my breath, "Why do you let people talk to you like that?" surprised at my shaking hands and the fury in my voice.

He looked at me, surprised. "Simple psychology, old sport. If I let her get to me, I give her power over me."

"What are you talking about? She just called you a limey fag."

"Quite. But as I am not, as she so delicately put it, a fag—and even if I were, I would take no offence, because there is no dishonour in being gay—no harm done."

"That's not the point, you moron. She insulted you. It doesn't bother you that she acts like you're a notch above swamp gas on the evolutionary chain?"

"Not a whit."

"Jeeze, you're something else. And what's this crap about her having power over you?"

"If I allow her to trouble me, she wins. If I take her seriously, I relinquish control of my life to her. Why should I give her the satisfaction?"

"But doesn't it piss you off when somebody takes a shot at you? Not that you don't *ask* for it, Mr. Spats-and-ascot-and-Queen's-English."

"Not at all," he said, ignoring my own jab and snapping his lock shut. "I simply consider the source."

How do you reason with someone like that?

Quinn, assistant head of the math department, was one of those teachers who thought that making kids look stupid was a way of motivating them. She was a thin, angular, black-haired crow, totally without a sense of humour. She tested us every Friday, and on Monday she stood at the front of the room, the blackboard behind her covered in formulas and equations, our graded tests cradled in one arm. She lectured us on the importance of discipline, slashing the air with her free hand as she rambled.

Then she handed out the tests. One at a time. Starting with the one that had the highest mark. As this ritual unfolded, the tension in the room was as thick as oil. She called out a name, the victim walked up to retrieve the work and returned to his or her desk. The first few kids she would greet with smiles, the middle group were rewarded with a blank face, and the final bunch—my group—got the cold Quinn stare.

On the first Monday of the semester Chumley got the top mark. And the second week. But that same day, after Quinn had finished her little humiliation exercise, Maddie, who always did fairly well, put up her hand.

"Yes, Maddie?"

"Do you HAVE to do this?" she asked. "I mean, couldn't you just hand the tests back in RANDOM ORDER or something?"

Murmurs of agreement rippled across the room, bringing a scowl to Quinn's already pinched face.

"The way you're doing it," Maddie rushed on, "it makes some of us feel REAL BAD."

"There's no reason to feel real*ly* bad," Quinn said. "If people feel real*ly* bad about their marks, they should study harder."

Phil tried to come to Maddie's rescue. "But aren't our marks private?" he asked.

"No, Mr. Lawyer, they are not. All of you," Quinn said to the class, "had better get used to this because, at mid-semester and after the final exams, your grades will be posted on the bulletin board. I'll say this one more time: if you want to feel better about your results, improve them."

During this exchange, I was watching Chumley. Quinn's methods were probably all right with him, I thought, since he had aced both tests so far. Chumley looked on, his face calm. It was impossible to know what he was thinking.

As he had the first week, he loaned his test to Phil and Maddie so they could see how he had arrived at the correct solutions. I took a gander too, even though I was hopeless in math. I was one of those Quinn wouldn't admit existed: I could study and practise until my teeth fell out and I would never ace a math test. I was lucky to pass.

Chumley's test paper was beautiful. You'd have sworn he had cheated. His answers came in the order the questions were given—he didn't do the easy ones first, as Quinn always suggested—and they were perfect. No corrections, just line after line of clear, neat, legible numbers and letters. He was so confident, he wrote the tests in ink. With a fountain pen.

But in the third week, something changed. Chumley came second in the Monday ritual, earning a sympathetic smile from Quinn, as if to say, I'll let you away with this only once. He hadn't done the last problem.

"What HAPPENED?" Maddie asked.

"Maybe old CN isn't perfect after all," I said.

Chumley smiled. "Not to worry, my dear," he said to Maddie.

The following Monday saw Chumley walking to the front of the class after five kids had gone up before him. Quinn didn't make eye contact with him. Chumley's test showed why. This time, he had left off two questions. But as before, the solutions he did complete were perfect.

"He's up to something," Phil said at lunch the same day, after Chumley had left for the library.

"Up to what?" I said. "So he didn't know the answers. It happens."

"Vic, the guy can knock over any problem you give him. I've seen him work. There's something going on."

"I don't buy it."

"Don't buy WHAT?" Maddie asked.

Chumley kept up the routine, and one day he got a special mention from Quinn. "For the first time in this class's dubious history," she said before she began her Monday routine, "someone actually got a zero!"

And after she had distributed all the tests except one, Chumley stood, buttoned his sports jacket, straightened his ascot, and walked forward. When he got to the front, Quinn wouldn't hand him his test.

"What do you mean by handing in a blank paper?" she demanded.

"The Scriptures," Chumley said, "admonish us that the first shall be last and the last, first."

A rare look of astonishment passed across Quinn's face. "I don't understand," she said.

"Apparently not," Chumley replied. Then he slid the paper from her hand and walked slowly back to his seat, his face as calm as a summer morning.

"That was beautiful!" Phil crowed around a mouthful of fries and gravy.

"Philip, I do wish you'd swallow your cud before speaking," Chumley said. "And thank you for the compliment."

"I STILL don't GET it," Maddie put in as she struggled with the cap on a bottle of juice.

"He got zero on purpose," I said. "Right?" I looked at Chumley, who just smiled that satisfied-cat smile of his.

"But THAT'S the part I don't GET!"

"As CN would say," Phil explained, "it's elementary, my dear. He's trying to teach

Quinn a lesson. He's been doing it in stages, getting a lower mark each week."

"WHAT LESSON?"

In a way, Quinn was like Maddie. She didn't get it. Or pretended she didn't. Her mean-spirited ritual continued.

One morning toward the end of the semester, I got to school late—not a rare thing for me, but this time it wasn't my fault. My bus had broken down. It was too far from home to go back and take the day off, too far from the school to walk. So we all had to wait until the company sent out another bus.

I got to school about halfway through the first period—English. I sauntered down the hall, enjoying the break in routine, climbed the stairs to the second floor where my locker was. Up there, every third locker had a sheet of paper taped to it. Some kind of Students' Council event, I figured, ignoring the sheet on the locker next to mine—Chumley's. I got my stuff and hurried into English.

The atmosphere in the class was, I don't know, *charged*. Things looked normal on the surface—Mr. Singh had everybody working on their independent studies. They were reading, making notes, drafting their research papers. I took my seat. Tammy, who sat next to me, looked up. Her eyes glittered with excitement. She stole a quick glance toward Singh, then slowly slid a sheet of paper from under her notebook. It was a list of some kind. Across the top, in a zany handwritten font I'd never seen before, it read, "Blue-Box Boogie."

"Alarm clock failure?" Singh's voice pulled me away from the list.

"Better than that, sir," I said. "The yellow monster died."

A few kids snickered.

"A masterful example of metaphor. I take it you mean a bus breakdown."

"Exactly," I replied.

Singh smiled. He was cool. Most of the time. "Feel ready for some heavy scholarship?"

"Got my stuff right here," I said. "Ernest Hemingway."

"Yuck," some girl at the back commented.

I opened my novel and pretended to read while I took a good look at the paper Tammy had given me.

I worked at a variety store after school and on weekends, so I knew an inventory when I saw one. And I had carried many blue recycling boxes to the alley behind the store. Along with notations for numbers of cans of soup and spaghetti sauce and sardines, jars of cheese spread and pickles and mayonnaise, I read line after line, stretching to the bottom of the page, listing the brand names of red and white wine, whisky and cans of imported beer. The titles of at least four gossip mags were there, too.

When I read the last line, I laughed out loud.

Singh looked up. "I had no idea that Papa H. was a humorist."

"Sorry, sir."

I looked again at the sentence. "Contents of the blue recycling box of Ms. J. Quinn over a two-week period. Compiled by the masked avenger."

I looked across the room to Chumley.

Math was next period, and I had never seen kids in such a hurry to get there. The word was out. When Quinn came through the door of the math office into the classroom, her face was without expression. But she had no tests under her arm.

She assigned a list of problems from the text-book, warned us to work quietly and returned to the office, leaving the door open a crack. There wasn't much math done. Whispers swished back and forth. The air of expectation built with every passing minute.

Quinn, it seemed, was a heavy drinker. Lots to gossip about there, but no big deal really. And she liked celebrity mags. So did half the girls in the school and probably some of the guys. I couldn't have cared less if Quinn went home every day, poured a whisky, put her feet up and lost herself in a gossip rag. But the thing was, in her lectures about hard work and discipline, Quinn was always putting down soap operas and comic books, labelling them trash for simpletons. The mathematical mind, she would say, is a disciplined mind, with no room for self-indulgence.

The class dragged, and Quinn didn't appear. Who put up the list? everybody wanted to know. In the swirl of talk around me, name after name was mentioned. But I knew who it was. I looked at Phil and he nodded. Even Maddie, intelligent-but-not-always-with-it Maddie, knew.

At the end of the period, after the bell rang, Quinn finally appeared, carrying a small cardboard carton. She set it on the corner of her desk.

"The quizzes are in there," she said. "Pick yours up on your way out."

The next week, Chumley aced his test.

"Care to join me in my humble repast, Vic?" Chumley asked in his nasal British twang as he unscrewed the cap of his thermos and poured a cup of steaming soup.

"No, thanks, I'll pass."

Chumley unwrapped his sandwich, cheese goo on whole wheat. "Speaking of which, shall you, do you think?"

It was the last week of classes before final exams. Phil and Maddie were already geared up, arranging study schedules. They and Chumley were very serious about doing well. And me? I went along for the ride. I wanted to pass, but that was all—just to avoid summer school.

"I don't know. I guess so."

"Your confidence and enthusiasm overwhelm."

"Yeah, well, I'm a humble guy."

"Indeed."

I picked up my burger and took a bite, watching Chumley eat. He held the spoon with his baby finger curled, dipped into the tomato soup, pushing the spoon away from him across the bowl, brought it to his mouth and sipped delicately. He had tried one day to get Phil to stop slurping, but that was a lost cause. Phil ate the way you'd shovel dirt into a hole.

Chumley was in tight with us now. Everybody tolerated him, kind of like a harmless crazy uncle living upstairs. Phil had accepted him long ago—"He's got style," he'd said—and it was clear to everyone but Chumley and Maddie that she was in love with him.

But I was still cautious. There was something about Chumley that got on my nerves—not the accent or the eccentric clothes, not the high marks. Not even the sense I still got that he considered himself a superior being. It was a kind of phoniness. He gave the impression he was rich and privileged, could have gone to a private school but chose not to—that kind of thing.

Maybe it was the clothes that gave him away. He wore a jacket and ascot, but it was the same jacket and ascot day after day. His shirt collars were sometimes frayed. His leather shoes, always polished, were worn down at the heels. He was trying to put one over on us, and nobody but me seemed to mind.

Following a trolley bus on a bicycle, especially at rush hour, is easy. One afternoon, from the shadows beside the school, I watched Chumley climb on board the A3, cane in one hand, his trusty briefcase in the other. A few minutes later, I zipped along half a block behind the bus as it headed deeper into the heart of the city, where the streets grew more crowded, narrower and dirtier, the mantis arms on the bus roof sparking on the overhead wires.

Finally, in a neighbourhood I wasn't familiar with, when the bus pulled away from the stop I saw Chumley standing on the sidewalk. He had taken off the spats and funny hat and he had put the cane away. Even the ascot was gone. Weaving among the shoppers, Chumley walked past a bank and some fruit and vegetable stands and pushed through the doors of a dollar store.

I waited for three changes of the traffic lights, then locked my bike to a parking meter and followed him in. I made my way carefully among aisles of plastic toys, watering cans, cheap knockoffs of watches, calculators and cameras. I spotted him at the back of the store. With a few aisles of men's clothing between us, I stood watching him.

A man came through a curtain at the back. He was dressed in grey coveralls and carried a mop in one hand and a bucket in the other. He smiled when he saw Chumley, nodded, and stashed the cleaning equipment in a closet.

Even before he spoke, I knew he was Chumley's father. He had the same fair hair (with a bit of grey), the same nose, the same slight build. But I was surprised when he said, "Hi, Charlie."

And shocked when I heard the reply. "Hi, Dad. Ready to go?"

Because it was said without the slightest trace of an accent.

The man removed a windbreaker from the closet, pulled it on and closed the door. They ambled out of the store together. I unlocked my bike and followed from a safe distance. Chumley-Charlie and his father strolled down the street and turned a corner, chatting away. They passed a church, a playground, an abandoned factory with boarded-up windows, then turned onto a street of rooming houses and decrepit bungalows. They entered a small house with a cracked cement porch. The place seemed to slump under its own weight as if it was sinking into the ground.

So the guy who had convinced all his teachers to call him Chumley was a fake. On my way home, pedalling against the spring wind, I tried to figure out how he had managed to change his name on the school records, then I remembered that on the first day of the semester, when he had dropped Chumley on my shoulders like a sack of potatoes, the principal never did say his name. The new kid had introduced himself as Chumley N. etcetera and we had believed him.

Why had Chumley-Charlie come all the way across town to our school? There must have been half a dozen closer to his house. Had he been thrown out of other places for bad behaviour? Had he flunked out? Not likely. And why the act—the accent, the barely concealed snobbery, the costume? It wasn't as if he had been trying all this time to blend in. I didn't have the answers, but I had discovered a few things. I knew where he came from, and I knew he was a phony. And I didn't intend to keep it a secret.

Friday was the last day of classes. On Monday exams would start, and after a week of agony we'd be free for the summer. In the hall after first period, Maddie came rushing toward me, clutching her books to her chest.

I said, "I've got something to—"

"We need to TALK, Vic," she gushed. "Meet me at my locker before lunch. It's IMPORTANT!" And she was gone in the stream of bodies.

I waited for her at the beginning of lunch period. I had been looking forward to giving her and Phil my news at the same time and bursting Chumley-Charlie's bubble in a dramatic announcement, but I'd have to change my plans and tell Maddie first.

She came charging down the hall. She spun the dial on her lock, yanked open her locker, dumped her books inside like an armful of unwanted garbage, slammed the door, snapped the lock closed and grabbed my arm.

"Come ON," she said, dragging me toward the doors to the playing field.

A few kids had already taken spots on the bleachers, munching sandwiches and crunching potato chips in the noonday sun. Maddie pulled me to the top row and sat down.

"OKAY," she said, letting out a deep breath. "Vic, I need to ASK you something. You have to PROMISE to be HONEST."

"Um, sure, Maddie. What's up?"

"You have to PROMISE," she repeated.

"Okay, okay. I promise. Even though I don't know what I'm promising."

Maddie's eyes sparkled and danced. She fixed me in her gaze and said, "What do you think about CHUMLEY? I mean, REALLY?"

The air rushed out of my lungs. Damn, I thought, she found out about him. She knows. So much for my big exposé. Before I could get a word out, she charged ahead.

"Because, I'm thinking of asking him to the PROM!"

"The prom? You're going to ask him to the prom?" I said stupidly.

"Is there an ECHO around here?" she said. "Come on, GRANDPA, dig the WAX out of your ears."

"Maddie, look. There's something you've got to know about Char— Chumley. I found out a few things."

Out on the field, a couple of guys were tossing a football back and forth, calling out to one another. Below us, someone had turned on a boom box, and some kind of classical music pounded out of it, so loud it put my nerves on edge.

"The MORE you can tell me, the BETTER," Maddie said. "Because I really LIKE him."

"Yeah, I know you do. That's why I have to tell you this."

"Tell me WHAT? Spit it OUT."

"Chumley is— Hey! You guys wanna turn that crap down a little?" I shouted. The boom box owner gave me the finger but lowered the volume anyway.

"Chumley LIKES that kind of music," Maddie said. "Now COME ON, Vic. What do you THINK?"

I pictured Chumley walking down the sidewalk behind his father to the peeling door of the run-down house on a street of run-down houses. I pictured his cane, his pathetic hat, his ridiculous briefcase, the ironic way he raised one eyebrow to make a silent comment about whatever was going on. I saw him sitting on the bus for an hour each morning, on his way to our school, putting on his costume as the bus neared his stop, composing himself for the daily routine in which he pretended to be someone else.

"Okay, Maddie. You asked. You're my friend, so I'm going to tell you the truth. Chumley is—"

"Come ON!"

"The thing is," I went on, "Chumley is . . . special. He's . . . well, kind of delicate."

"You mean, like, SENSITIVE?"

"Yeah."

"I KNOW. It's one of the things I LIKE about him. He's not afraid to be sensitive."

"Yeah, that's it exactly. So, what I mean is, at first, he might not seem like he wants to go to the prom with you. But I'm sure he does."

Maddie's smile seemed to make her freckles vibrate. "You're SURE?"

"I'm certain."

"THANKS, Vic. I KNEW I could count on you!"

I was at my locker, stuffing books into my backpack for the weekend study grind. Chumley bounced down the hall, lowered his briefcase to the floor and opened his locker.

"Greetings, my good man," he said.

"Hey, CN."

"Girded your loins for the exams, yet, old sport?"

"You know, CN, one of these days it would be nice to know what you're talking about."

He laughed. "Quite so."

"Look," I began. "I was wondering. Any way you'd be willing to give me a hand prepping for the math exam?"

Up went the eyebrow. Chumley's eyes searched my face, hunting for sarcasm. Then he smiled. "Certainly, old thing. Delighted."

I nodded. "That'd be great. And one other thing. Maddie is going to ask you to the prom."

His mouth dropped open, and for the first time since I'd met him, Chumley betrayed surprise. "The prom? Me?" As fast as he'd let his mask slip, he had it back in place. "Indeed?" he said.

"Yeah, indeed. And listen, old sport, old chap, old thing, do yourself a favour."

"What would that be?"

"Say yes."

the promise

(for Molly Macdonald)

<pre>
 FROM: Cole Ingram
          <cole.ingram@freemail.net>
SUBJECT: bulletin from brother
   TO: Marci
          <pianogir134@tormail.com>
 DATE: April 4, 1:48 PM EDT
</pre>

Dear Marci,

God. I'm here, finally. Sweaty and exhausted, joints and muscles screaming in protest. What a trip. Bad enough that Shel gave me *one* day's notice, with no time to assemble the proper gear for a job in a place I've never been and know nothing about. The plane was late leaving the city, which made me miss my connecting flight, which meant a two-hour wait in the airport lounge, jet-lagged and rumpled, before the short hop to Edinburgh.

Anyway, here I am, at the hotel, a nice little place I'll tell you about later. Just wanted you to know I've arrived safe and (almost) sound.

—Cole

PS I have great news!

FROM: Cole Ingram
<cole.ingram@freemail.net>
SUBJECT: **the good news**
TO: Marci
<pianogir134@tormail.com>
DATE: April 5, 2:43 AM EDT

Hi.

It's past midnight. Had a little nap before I cabbed into the city for dinner. (The hotel is on the Comiston Road south of the city's centre. The room is tiny; Shel warned me, but I didn't think he meant *this* small.) Went to bed early, but woke up in the middle of the night. My body's clock is off by five hours.

So: the news. Shel and I were settled in (two hours late) at cruising altitude, holding our overpriced drinks, when he turned to me and suggested, Let's have a toast. He raised his glass, his mammoth diamond ring glinting, and said, To our new director.

I choked on my drink and spluttered, Excuse me? Shel grinned. Turns out I'm not a "location scout," meaning glorified gofer, any more. They liked the trailer I did (all five seconds of it) for the latest Icebitch video.

(You know, Adele Deigle, who sings in underwear and chains? Who pretends she writes her own songs, but doesn't?) They've always appreciated my eye for atmosphere and detail when I search out locations—so much so they never wanted to move me. But they realize they have to give me a chance or they're going to lose me. I'm talented. I'm dedicated. Great future in rock videos. Blah, blah.

I was thinking, as Shel swallowed most of his scotch in one gulp, Who died? Whose shoes am I being asked to fill until they can get somebody else? I asked Shel exactly that.

Nobody died, he laughed. What's this about shoes? We want you to direct the kick-off video for "Spirit and Stone." There ought to be lots of great locations in an old city like Edinburgh. All those cemeteries. Castles. Donjons, maybe. Torture machines. Now, instead of just finding great venues for us, you'll run the show.

So, your big bro is a director now! This could be the break I've been waiting for, after years of slogging. Okay, it's not the world-changing documentaries I dreamed of making back in high school (and ever since). But who knows, maybe rock videos are the

first step toward bigger things. Let's hope.
God, what a business! No wonder it drives
me nuts sometimes.

—Love, Cole

PS I'll try really hard to be home in time for
your birthday. You made me swear to it, but
things have changed.

FROM: Cole Ingram
<cole.ingram@freemail.net>
SUBJECT: **wired**
TO: Marci
<pianogir134@tormail.com>
DATE: April 5, 8:32 PM EDT

Hi, Marci,

Crazy day today. I'm exhausted, exhilarated, wired on coffee, buzzing with adrenaline—and scared. Stop being dramatic, I hear you saying. Read on, sister.

Spent a couple of hours last night riffling through my tour books and visit-Scotland pamphlets. Got up early and took a cab across the Firth of Forth to Dunfermline. There's a cathedral there with a ruined abbey, and that was my destination.

All this is hush-hush right now, so don't breathe a word, but Adele is going to do a one-off collaboration CD with Ghost Girls, one of the hot new ghoul bands. Most of their songs are about death in some way. Now, dear sister, kindly return your rolled eyes to the forward position. Remove the sneer from your face. You, of the classical piano. The gurus at the label think Adele's feisty in-your-face attitude and GG's neo-gothic mysticism will be a dynamite mix. The lead song is "Don't Need God No More." It's going to make a lot of noise—in more ways than one. A real put-down of faith and religion. Hence the tumbledown ancient abbey. Sort of symbolizes the theme of the song. Subtle, eh?

Anyway, it was a sunny day and the abbey ruins, with their carefully tended lawns and flower beds and walkways, were, well, too nice. But given the right weather and angles, along with the usual digital magic on the computer, we should be able to do something for Adele. I spent the better part of the day taking pix while a peacock dragged his fan across the lawn and squawked.

In the late afternoon I took the cab back into Edinburgh where I had a cappuccino and made a few notes on my map. I was hunting for more churches, because churches mean cemeteries, and I wanted lots more than the abbey ruins.

Turns out there were more burial grounds within a mile radius of my cappuccino than you could shake a bone at. St. Cuthbert's graveyard had lots of potential but it's too, I don't know, peaceful. Refined, almost. Far down along Princes Street, Calton Cemetery, on the edge of the vale, walled, gravel paths and grass, large headstones, tombs and something I wasn't familiar with, mural monuments. That's a grave with a part of the perimeter wall as its headstone.

Anyway, Calton is too small, so, more walking under a sky that had gone all cloudy and grey, more cemeteries, until I crossed the George Four bridge and stumbled upon the Greyfriars Kirkyard. Kirk meaning church. And this place was a treasure trove.

If you'd tried to design the perfect venue for a horror movie—or a ghoul-rock video— you couldn't do better. The place was established in 1532! Like Calton, it's enclosed by a wall. You turn off Candlemakers Row, pass under a stone arch and step back almost 500 years. The ancient church hunkers on the brow of a low hill.

I was alone. I could hear light traffic out on Candlemakers Row, and disembodied voices floating in from somewhere. Long shadows striped the gravel paths and grass—all soaked from an afternoon shower. Right away, I felt in my bones—so to speak—that there was something that made Greyfriars special, in some way unlike the other burial yards I'd visited that day. A sort of calm. A sense of, I don't know, expectation.

And a feeling of doom.

No, I'm *not* being dramatic.

Maybe I was just tired from a long day's research, but suddenly I had to struggle for breath, as if something was squeezing my chest. The place was nothing like cemeteries at home, with neat rows of headstones and a park-like atmosphere that tries too hard to deny the fact that dead people are decomposing under your feet. In Greyfriars, death is *triumphant*. It's right in your face. It has attitude. There are skull-and-crossbones and skeletons carved on some monuments— and they're *grinning*, as if to say, Ha! Gotcha! There are devils' faces, leering, with mouths wide open, tongues sticking out. A chubby baby angel with a skull on its knee (I'm not kidding, Marci). The torso of a crowned skeleton, rib cage jutting out from under a ragged shawl.

I began to explore, with every step firming my decision that this was the locale for GG's video. I took stills and clips as I went, and, as the afternoon gave in to evening, got the best of all horror effects, ground mist. I strolled slowly along the sloping path to the right of the church. The gravel crunched underfoot, the thickening mist flowed around my legs, cold and damp, and even in the flat light the moisture on the tombstones glistened. My stomach churned. The feeling that I was being watched crept up my spine.

Recording the scene as I moved along, I worked my way behind the church and up a path next to the wall monuments. A devil's face glowered malevolently, as if to say, What are *you* doing here? On the higher ground, the fog was a little thinner. I turned around and captured the lower half of the graveyard on video. Then I trudged up toward the southwest corner of the cemetery.

I could make out a wrought-iron fence, chained and padlocked. Behind it, an open space, about ten metres wide, a sort of corridor between tombs. Was it the mist, or was something moving there? I cursed. On the other side of the fence lay a bundle of clothing or something, ruining the shot. I stepped nearer to remove it. There was a small sign on the fence, but I couldn't quite make out the words.

A chill breeze stirred the fog, and I could see the object more clearly.

It wasn't a bundle of clothes. It was a man, stretched out on the bare wet ground.

I inched closer. The attitude in which he lay, the outstretched legs and arms, the absolute stillness of him, told me he was dead. He was bearded, his face filthy, hair matted with mud. His cheek was mashed against the bars, and his open eyes seemed to stare through them. Specks of dirt were stuck on one eyeball. His heavy boots had gouged trenches in the soil. His arms stretched through the bars, and his fingers had clawed furrows in the dirt. It seemed that he had been so terrified by something that he had tried to scrabble *between* the bars.

The horror etched on his face sent a chill creeping into my bones. I snapped his picture before I turned and ran.

Within two minutes I was out on the street, gasping for breath. A bus churned past in the fading light. Car tires hissed on the damp pavement. A woman hustled by, pushing a baby carriage. I pulled out my phone and keyed in the emergency number, reported the body and the location to the operator, who took my name and told me to stay put. No chance. A few minutes later, I hailed a passing taxi and I fled to the warmth and light of my hotel.

FROM: Cole Ingram
       <cole.ingram@freemail.net>
SUBJECT: **strange!**
TO: Marci
     <pianogir134@tormail.com>
DATE: April 6, 4:27 PM EDT

Dear Marci,

The police just left.

I spent last night thrashing around in my bed, trying to make myself fall asleep, pushing thoughts and images out of my head, telling myself I wasn't afraid. Marci, I've seen dead bodies before—on TV, at our parents' funerals. But as bad as that was, it was nothing like the corpse I stumbled onto at Greyfriars, with his limbs outstretched and reaching, his face twisted in horror. I got up early and went for a walk to clear my head. And as I walked, I wondered, why had no one responded to my emergency call?

I was in my room, staring out at the rain, calming my nerves with a cup of strong tea, when the knock came. I opened the door to find a skinny guy, jacket and tie under his raincoat, the smell of cigarettes on his clothes. Inspector Braid, he said, flashing his ID. I let him in and gave him the only chair in the room, while I perched awkwardly on the edge of the bed.

He asked to see my passport, inquired politely how I liked Edinburgh. What did I do for a living? Must be an interesting occupation, working with recording stars, travelling, making videos. I had the feeling he already knew what I was telling him, that he'd checked up on me before coming.

All the time he was making small talk, his eyes flicked around the room like a housefly that couldn't decide where to land. So you're here researching locations for your work? he said, even though we'd been over all that. Yes, I told him, again. For music celebrities, he said. Yeah, you could call them that, I said, wondering what this guy would think of Adele with her eyebrow rings and nose studs and skimpy clothing.

Then, as his eyes lit on the cameras on my dresser top, he said, I suppose a bit of publicity wouldn't come amiss. Focus attention on your project, like.

Publicity? I asked.

He twiddled one of the buttons on the sleeve of his jacket. What with your, er, theme, as it were, so much like our City of the Dead here in Edinburgh.

You've lost me, I told him.

You've not heard of the City of the Dead? The underground tours through ancient passageways and cellars along the Royal Mile?

I noticed some ads on the sides of buses, I said. I thought it was a musical or a movie.

No, it's a tourist attraction, he sniffed. The guided walk through Greyfriars Kirkyard is the most popular part. All that nonsense about hauntings and so on. You've not heard of it, then?

Look, I said, confused and a little ticked, I don't know what you're talking about. I thought you were here about my phone call. The, um, body I saw.

Well, he said with a thin smile, that's just the rub, Mr. Ingram. It seems there is no body.

My cup bonked the rug between my feet. What! I heard myself exclaim.

The smarmy grin fell away and his voice firmed up. A thorough search of the area turned up nothing, he said, but an old black coat and a few empty beer bottles—probably left behind by youngsters. They sometimes like to have the odd party at Greyfriars. I want to emphasize, Mr. Ingram, that we don't take mischievous reports lightly. We—

You think my call was a hoax? I cut in. That I made it all up?

I'm telling you there was nothing there.

I know what I saw, I insisted. The man was dead. He couldn't have just gotten up and walked away.

The cop heaved himself out of the chair, buttoned his jacket and raincoat. Well, he said wearily, we'll put it down to your overactive artistic imagination, shall we?

And he left. End of investigation.

Shaking with anger, I retrieved my tea mug from the floor and poured some scotch. Had I imagined the whole thing? I went to the window and watched the cop drive away in the rain.

FROM: Cole Ingram
                <cole.ingram@freemail.net>
SUBJECT: **doubts**
TO: Marci
                <pianogir134@tormail.com>
DATE: April 7, 6:45 AM EDT
ATTACHMENTS: **corpse?.jpg**

It took only a few minutes to download the stills and movie clips from my cameras to the laptop.

I'm good at my work, I know that. My pictures captured the menacing mood of Greyfriars so well I began to fidget as I went through them, to hear imaginary noises in the walls and at the window. I relived the clammy afternoon, the spooky mist, the silent graves, the atmosphere of doom. The sense of being watched—more than that—inspected by the doleful marble eyes of the devils and angels on the tombs.

I examined the shots closely—the pan of the whole kirkyard, the wall monuments grey and wet in the mist—and noticed something that hadn't registered when I had the camera up to my eye. Carved into one of the monuments was some text under the words Covenanters'

Memorial. Who or what was a covenanter? I asked myself.

Then came the pix of the iron bars, the long corridor that stretched between the mural tombs into the mist, the innocuous sign, white letters on black, illegible in fog and fading light. I zoomed in on the sign. Covenanters' Prison, it said. Who ever heard of a jail in a cemetery?

The next shot showed the man lying stiff as marble, face jammed against the bars, arms desperately reaching, fingers clawing the dirt.

He was there, all right.

Or was he? I sat back, took a few deep breaths, shook the tension from my shoulders, tried to look at the photo objectively, as if I was seeing it for the first time. I know a camera lens can be stark in its truthfulness, but it can also give a perspective that will lead to different conclusions. Change the angle, change the light, and you have a different effect. And I had to admit that, if I asked a stranger, What do you see here? he might say, A body, but he might also admit, I can't say for sure.

Had someone played a trick on me? Some of the kids the cop had mentioned? Was it a drunk, sleeping it off? Inspector Braid had insisted that there was no cadaver.

He was wrong. The rictus of horror on the corpse's face, the dirt on his eyeball, couldn't be denied.

I tried a digital examination of the photo, enlarging and diminishing sections, but I got nowhere. I threw myself on the bed. Why was I doubting my own senses? I asked myself. When I was in Greyfriars I had seen the corpse of a man who died a terrible, painful death.

Then I remembered the cop had also mentioned hauntings.

Marci, I can see your eyes rolling again, and hear that exasperated Tsk! of yours. Just bear with me here. What could it hurt, I asked myself, to look into the matter?

So I'm going on line to do some searching.

FROM: Cole Ingram
<cole.ingram@freemail.net>
SUBJECT: **discoveries**
TO: Marci
<pianogir134@tormail.com>
DATE: April 7, 10:12 AM EDT
ATTACHMENTS: **martyrsmonument.jpg**

Dear Marci,

Had the "fry-up" in cholesterol city, the hotel dining room. I was starved. I'd stayed up late doing research, gotten up early to continue.

Here's what I found out. I started with "Covenanters." There was lots of info on the Net, and most of the websites were right here in Scotland. Some condensed history here, so hang on. King Charles I of Scotland wanted to continue the work begun by his father, James, in amalgamating the Church of Scotland with the Church of England, so in 1637 he had the Book of Common Prayer introduced and proclaimed that anyone who didn't follow it was an enemy of the state. Punishment? You guessed it. Death.

It seems strange nowadays, but back then the king thought he ruled by God's permission (and therefore was always right), and the Church was "established," i.e., the official religion of the country with the king as its head. Catholics and other dissenting Protestants like the Presbyterians did not accept the official church.

A group of Presbyterians were incensed at Chuck One's arrogance and tyranny. Only Jesus Christ, they believed, could be head of the church. They wrote up an agreement or pact (the National Covenant) in 1638, promising to oppose the B of CP. They all signed it. And, my dear Marci, guess where they nailed up the covenant?

On the door of Greyfriars Kirk.

For many years afterwards, the covenanters were aggressively persecuted and, after a particularly hot battle in 1679, more than a thousand were jailed at Greyfriars. Thus, the Covenanters' Prison. Eventually, many of them were hanged, just because they refused to use the king's book. No wonder the place has such an eerie atmosphere.

After I had read all this, I sat back and mulled it all over. What would it be like to live in a place where my religion was illegal? What if I had to sign an oath saying I *didn't* believe in it, or I'd be hanged? Except for you and maybe a couple of other people, there is nothing that I would give my life for. What would it be like to believe in something so much you were willing to put your life on the line?

The covenanters fought battles and suffered persecution, and many died for the right to worship freely. Was the man I saw at Greyfriars one of them?

FROM: Cole Ingram
<cole.ingram@freemail.net>
SUBJECT: **hauntings**
TO: Marci
<pianogir134@tormail.com>
DATE: April 7, 12:31 PM EDT

Dear Marci,

I just came back from a walk in the little park across the road from the hotel. I did a lot of thinking.

And I asked around the hotel—the chambermaid, a waiter in the cafe, the woman at the desk—about the ghost stories. It's amazing how much credence is given to the notion that "there must be something to it." Up in my room, I went on the Net again. All kinds of newspaper reports and articles allege that evil spirits have caused poltergeist-type events at the kirkyard, and this has been going on for centuries. Psychics routinely sense the "presence" of spirits in the area, especially on the left side of the prison (where I saw the man's body, by the way—a little detail I didn't notice at the time). Visitors on the City of the Dead tours regularly report feeling oppressed and sick to their stomachs in the kirkyard, just as I had. Others go so far as to say they have difficulty breathing and think they are suffocating. Local clergy have tried exorcisms at Greyfriars. Unsuccessfully, it seems.

I could hardly believe what I was reading. Apparently normal, apparently credible people in Edinburgh believe there are spirits haunting the Greyfriars Kirkyard.

And apparently I'm one of them.

FROM: Cole Ingram
       <cole.ingram@freemail.net>
SUBJECT: **City of the Dead**
TO: Marci
    <pianogir134@tormail.com>
DATE: April 7, 9:06 PM EDT

Dear Marci,

I went back to Greyfriars. I had to, although I could hear your calm, reasonable voice telling me I was being ridiculous.

It was sunny and warm, and the daffodils on the hillside below Edinburgh Castle blazed like a golden grassfire. Candlemakers Row was sunlit, and a few tourists were wandering in the kirkyard when I got there. I made my way toward the prison, encountering a tour group on the way. Mostly young people, their anoraks open with the warmth of the afternoon, their hiking boots crunching on the gravel path. The tour guide was dressed in black.

I want to caution you, I heard him say in hushed tones, as we approach the jail. Over the years there have been many reports of visitors experiencing rather dire physical manifestations. Some have been knocked over, and a few actually knocked out.

Oohs and aahs from his audience.

But no one has been injured, the guide continued, at least, not yet. This way, please.

I let the pack move on ahead, then followed them to the prison gate. Everyone feeling all right? the guide inquired. Halfhearted murmurs of assent from the tourists. I searched the faces nearest me. His theatrical patter really had them hooked.

The spirit energy in Greyfriars, the guide went on, almost whispering, is by far the most potent on the entire City of the Dead tour. It is not at all unusual to experience foul odours—rotting flesh, offal, filth and so on. The spirit most often seen or felt is that of Lord Advocate George Mackenzie, a particularly cruel magistrate who delighted in sending many covenanters to the gallows. According to legend, he torments the jailed covenanters even after death, right here in the prison. As you file past the gate, you can take a look into the prison area before we move on.

After a few moments, the group followed him behind the church and down the hill, leaving me standing in the sun at the chained and padlocked gate.

I looked into the sun-drenched prison area just as the others had. Around me, birdsong and the sigh of the breeze in the trees that shaded parts of the kirkyard.

Nothing happened. Nothing appeared.

Were there grooves in the now dry dirt where the iron fence met the ground? Claw marks made by grasping human hands? Gouges dug by scrabbling boots? You could say so.

Or you could say not.

FROM: Cole Ingram
   <cole.ingram@freemail.net>
SUBJECT: **voices**
TO: Marci
                           <pianogir134@tormail.com>
DATE: April 8, 1:41 PM EDT

Dear Marci,

Just after lunch, a package arrived by courier from Shel in London. There were two large glossies inside, and a note. Costumes for Adele and the Ghost Girls, the memo said. I'd like your opinion. I think they're great. Call me soon as.

For "Don't Need God No More" Adele would be wearing a lacy halter top that showed lots of her implanted cleavage, and low-slung seventies-style bell-bottom jeans with religious symbols all over them. Each symbol was enclosed in a red ring with a diagonal line through it. The Ghost Girls, with long straight black hair and white death-mask makeup, wore ankle-length see-through robes slit from neck to navel.

I pictured Adele shouting out her song like a five-year-old in the grip of a tantrum at the abbey ruins in Dunfermline. GG half-naked, cavorting near the Covenanters' Prison gates. And a little voice I hadn't heard from in a long time started to natter away at the back of my mind.

In a place where people who had signed an oath to oppose the destruction of their religious freedom, I was planning to make a video that used bare skin and disrespect to sell CDs.

Oh, of course I knew that sex and disrespect were what GG and Adele aka Icebitch were all about. I also knew that our business isn't about respect or reverence. It's about *effect*—making a splash, gaining attention. And getting attention is harder and harder these days. Elvis used to do it with a greasy duck's-ass hairdo and a few hip thrusts. Nowadays you need lots more. Our market is kids, and when you're selling stuff to kids—music, clothes, sports—getting attention means two things: sex and disrespect. Sex plus disrespect equals money. And money talks.

Money doesn't talk, the little voice said, it swears.

•

FROM: Cole Ingram
<cole.ingram@freemail.net>
SUBJECT: **the message**
TO: Marci
<pianogir134@tormail.com>
DATE: April 9, 8:52 PM EDT

Dear Marci,

Who called three o'clock in the morning the long night of the soul? F. Scott Fitzgerald? I forget. Doesn't matter.

Forgive me for sounding dramatic. Last night I couldn't sleep. The old brain was in overdrive, with images charging around like demented kids in a toy store. Fog, mouldy stone walls, barefoot young women mouthing the words to songs, dead bodies. Around three I got up and sat at the window, sipping scotch and looking onto Comiston Road and mulling over the events of the past couple of days.

Marci, Greyfriars *is* haunted.

Not by the "spirit energy" mentioned by that tour guide. By things that are real—injustice, suffering, terror. All those people, jailed and starved and beaten and hanged by the neck—all for a little book, at the whim of a king who thought, like so many other rulers, that God talked through his mouth. Women and men and children hounded and persecuted for the way they prayed. People who have been forgotten.

And the dead man I saw stretched out on the wet ground? Was he imaginary? A trick of light and mist and fatigue? A ghost? Was it too fanciful to suppose that he was there to tell me something? Let's say—just for argument—that he showed himself to me, only me, to pass on a message. What would that message be?

Remember.

See, Marci? I'm way past wondering and worrying about whether the man I saw was real. I got the message.

Remember.

I can't shoot my video in that place.

FROM: Cole Ingram
<cole.ingram@freemail.net>
SUBJECT: **the promise**
TO: Marci
<pianogir134@tormail.com>
DATE: April 9, 11:04 PM EDT

Dear Marci,

I feel as if I've set down a heavy burden.

I took a long hot shower, dressed and sent for coffee and scones. While I had breakfast I read "The Scotsman," the newspaper that came with the coffee.

Marci, not much has changed since the Covenant was nailed to the Greyfriars church doors. In the newspaper there were reports of three wars in Africa. And the always-war in the Middle East. And the persecution of people around the globe because of their religion, or ethnic group, or gender. Before I had rolled up the paper and tossed it into the waste bin, I had made two decisions.

I will fulfill my obligation to Shel and make the video. But in St. Cuthbert's or Calton, not Greyfriars. Afterwards, I'll resign.

And I will try to find a way to make the kind of documentaries I've always dreamed of

doing but never had the courage to try. I
know it sounds pretentious, but I don't care:
it's about time I did something important.

But first I'm flying home for your
birthday. After all, a promise is a promise.

—Love, Cole

beer can man

Albert woke to the *clink* of his grandfather's Zippo. He burrowed deeper under the covers and pictured the silver lighter, almost lost in the old man's callused hand as he flipped back the lid with his thumb and flicked the tiny wheel for a spark. Albert saw the flame lifted to the cigarette between thin lips, the red glow swelling, the ash lengthening in front of the curling smoke. *Clink* as the lighter's lid snapped shut. He heard a throaty cough, and tobacco smoke filled the room.

Albert sat up, knuckling sleep from his eyes, and climbed out of bed. He straightened the bedclothes before rolling the cot under the chesterfield that filled the end wall of the single-wide. He pulled on the drawstring to raise the venetian blinds and looked out the window. Flat grey light flowed from a low, steel-coloured sky. Frost rimed the lanes between the mobile homes, the garbage cans beside the driveway, the neighbours' cars.

He padded to the kitchen nook where his grandfather sat at the table, his mug of tea before him. The Zippo rested atop a small green box of cigarette papers, which in turn sat on a matching packet of Macdonald's tobacco. Albert poured tea for himself, added milk and two spoons of sugar and sat down opposite his grandfather. Still half asleep, he stared at the picture of the young woman on the tobacco packet. Blond curls flowed from under her tam, and the clan plaid was draped over her shoulder. Albert had always suspected that his grandfather smoked Export because his family name was Macdonald.

"Might be our last trip of the year," his grandfather commented, looking out the window into the November sky. "They're calling for snow tomorrow or the day after."

Albert stirred his tea to cool it, then took a sip.

"How many slices?" the old man asked, getting to his feet.

"Two, please."

"Kinda jam?"

"Strawberry, I guess."

Albert's grandfather put the bread in the toaster and took a jar of jam from the fridge. "Looks like Cuddy will be able to play tonight after all," he said.

"Great. Now the Leafs will win for sure."

"Wouldn't bet on it."

Grandad was a Habs fan, but Albert loved the Leafs. The two of them never missed *Hockey Night in Canada*. Next Saturday, the Leafs and Montreal played at Toronto, and Albert and his grandfather would rib each other all through the game. His mom, who disliked hockey and complained good-naturedly every week that her TV was commandeered for the evening, would make popcorn.

"Where's Mom?" Albert asked, blowing on his tea.

"Workin'. That big stone house on Birchgrove Lane."

"Oh."

"You'll have to eat quick like," the old man said, stuffing his cigarette makings into the pocket of his flannel shirt. "We need to pick her up at noon. She said she'd be done cleaning by then."

Albert climbed into the pickup truck through the driver's side and slid along the seat. An accident a few years before had permanently jammed the passenger door. Albert's grandfather hauled himself behind the steering wheel, slammed the door and turned the key. "Here's hopin'," he muttered. The starter motor wheezed weakly, the engine coughed a couple of times, then held. He eased the truck into gear. It shuddered as it rolled out of the trailer park.

"Truck's more gutless every day. I think one of them pistons is just goin' around for the ride."

"Yeah, sounds like it," Albert said.

The old man headed toward the big highway that bypassed the town of Langdon. He turned onto a ramp, rounded the cloverleaf and, instead of merging into the light Saturday-morning traffic, pulled off onto the shoulder and parked under a bridge.

"Cans or bottles?" he asked, opening the door.

"Bottles, I guess," Albert replied.

"Thought it was my turn."

Last weekend, Albert had noticed his grandfather struggling with his sack, breathing more heavily than usual. The aluminum cans were much lighter than the bottles.

"I like doing the bottles."

"Suit yourself."

Albert and his grandfather grabbed burlap sacks from a heap in the back of the truck. Albert stuffed three of them inside his jacket and unrolled two more. The old man took one, and they set off. Eyes trained on the dry grass, they slowly made their way along the ditch beside the road, the old man picking up beer cans, the boy carefully placing beer bottles in one bag and soft drink bottles in the other. A raw wind stung Albert's face, and soon his hands were red and cold. He wished he had brought his gloves. But his grandfather never wore gloves on their Saturday pickups, so Albert didn't either.

Cars swooshed by, tires singing; trucks shifted down for the long hill. In the intervals between, Albert heard his grandfather's laboured breathing. He checked his pace. If he wasn't careful, he would unconsciously leave the old man behind. His grandfather walked slowly, dragging the potato sack behind him, bending carefully to pick up his prizes, sometimes dropping one because he had arthritis in his left thumb and it didn't work too well. "Like that damn old truck," he would say.

The bypass that circled the town was four kilometres long, divided evenly into one-kilometre sections by bridges. Each Saturday, Albert and his grandfather walked one of the sections, covering the entire bypass once a month.

Albert allowed his mind to wander as he searched the dead brown grass for bottles. He turned his head when an eighteen-wheeler thundered by and caught sight of the driver's shoulder through the side window. What would it be like to sit up there and go for miles and miles, every day a new and different destination? Maybe Grandad would let him drive the truck again today. For the past few weekends they had found a quiet spot on a country road and Albert had struggled with the stiff clutch and crabby gear shift, his veins buzzing with excitement.

As he walked, bent, stood, walked some more, accompanied by the faint clink of bottles in the bag he dragged behind him, eyes squinting against the chilly wind, Albert imagined the warm comfort of Renée's Cafe and a steaming plate of french fries smothered in gravy, fried beef and onions, peas and melted cheese. A glass of pop, beaded with condensation.

"Cherry cola?" his grandfather would always ask.

"Yup."

"Fries with the works, I suppose."

"Yup," Albert would answer, then watch his grandfather roll a smoke as they waited for their orders. The snack was their reward for the morning's work. His grandfather put the remainder of the money away "for a rainy day."

After a while, man and boy reached the next bridge and leaned their bulging sacks against the concrete. Albert's grandfather sat on his, pulled out his makings and rolled a cigarette. *Clink, clink* went the Zippo.

At length they hid the sacks in the bushes beside the bridge and waited for a break in the traffic before they made their way across the highway. They took up their work again, using the sacks Albert had kept inside his jacket. He had cooled off a little during the break, and the thin cloth of his coat was no match for the damp wind. His grandfather was moving more slowly during this second leg, so Albert took his time. It was ten o'clock before they found themselves opposite their truck on the far side of the highway.

They propped the bulging sacks against one another, crossed once more, and drove along the shoulder to retrieve the sacks they had hidden in the bushes. They took the exit ramp, crossed the bridge and headed in the opposite direction, stopping to pick up the second set of sacks. A big circle, Albert thought. Every Saturday we spend the morning making a big circle.

The old man and the boy visited three local parks, rooting through the trash barrels for bottles and cans, but at this time of year the yield was small. When they had checked every barrel in the third park, they took their sacks and some empty cartons from the truck and, on the scarred top of a picnic table, transferred the pop and beer bottles to the cartons.

"Not, bad," Albert's grandfather said when they had finished and Albert had hiked the boxes into the truck bed. "We filled all six cartons. That's—"

"Seven twenty," Albert said. "Not counting the cans."

His grandfather grunted. "Knew I brought you along for a reason."

They drove to a supermarket at the edge of town and, while his grandfather sat in the truck smoking and listening to the radio, Albert carried the two cartons of pop bottles into the store and waited patiently until the cashier was free to redeem them.

"Have a nice day, Albert," she said, handing over a few bills and counting out the coins.

"Thanks. You too."

"Guess everybody's stocking up for the hockey game tonight," Albert's grandfather commented as he pulled into the crowded parking lot of the beer store and slipped into a spot by the doors. There was a lineup inside the store.

The old man pulled on the handle and leaned his shoulder against the door to force it open. He went around to the back of the truck while Albert fetched a shopping cart. They loaded empty bottles on the cart and Albert wheeled it into the crowded store, followed by his grandfather dragging the sacks of beer cans. They queued up under the Returns sign, along with half a dozen men.

A few moments later, Albert had collected the bottle money and returned to the truck to wait for his grandfather. He turned on the radio and spun the dial to find his favourite station, but got only static. The car next to him backed away and a full-ton diesel "doolie" pulled in. Albert let out a low whistle and gazed at the shiny candy-apple red hood, the polished chrome grille surmounted by a gleaming statuette of a charging mountain sheep. The powerful diesel rumbled and clattered for a moment, then fell silent. A young man in black denim shirt and pants hopped out and went into the store.

With nothing else to do, Albert watched the customers. The lineup inside the store lengthened. A woman emerged, carrying a six-pack in her two hands as if it weighed ten kilograms. A man in a baseball jacket followed soon after, pushing a cart laden with cases of beer—all the same brand. Albert wondered what beer tasted like, what all the fuss was about.

A while later, the man in black came out, a case on one hip. He hefted the box into the back of the pickup and opened his door.

"What the hell was the holdup?" his buddy asked, flicking a cigarette butt out his window.

"Ah, some old fart in there, counting out empties, dropping them all over the friggin' place."

"Oh, him. Yeah, that's his wreck, the one with the hillbilly kid in it."

Albert fixed his gaze on the dashboard, on the hole where the cigarette lighter used to be.

"Pathetic," the man in black commented, slamming his door. "Friggin' welfare bum. Friggin' beer can man."

The big engine roared to life and the truck backed away.

Albert could see into the store. Saw his grandfather's back as he stood to the side of the Returns counter, waiting for the clerk to count the empties as he put them into boxes. Saw the tattered windbreaker, the baggy pants with the frayed cuffs, the boots broken at the heels. Saw the men in the queue staring at him, exchanging glances.

Hurry up, Albert whispered under his breath. Hurry up.

Finally the clerk handed some bills to Albert's grandfather. As the old man came through the door he caught Albert's eye, held up the bills and smiled. Albert shifted his gaze, looked out his window at the compact car that had replaced the red truck. There was a furry white dog in the back seat, his tongue lolling.

Albert's grandfather climbed into the truck, pulled the door closed and turned the key. "Here's hoping," he said softly. The truck's engine struggled to life, and the old man backed away.

"All right," he said. "We've got time before we pick your mom up. We've got a few bucks in our jeans. Let's hit the café. I know they've got a plate of fries-with-the-works there with your name on it."

"I'm not hungry," Albert said.

"Eh?"

"I don't want to go to the restaurant. And I don't want to drive this stupid goddamn no-good truck, and I don't want to pick through garbage at the park any more!"

"What are you talkin' about? What's the matter?"

Albert stared through the cracked windshield, wishing he could explain.

On Thursday, his grandfather, who hadn't been himself all week, went to bed early. Albert cleared the supper dishes while his mother wiped down the table and swept the floor. When they had finished, his mother said, "Sit down for a second, Albert."

Albert pulled up a chair, watching as his mother opened a cupboard and reached to the top shelf. She placed a small envelope on the table and sat down.

"Take a look," she said, pushing a wisp of hair from her eyes.

"It's addressed to Grandad," he said.

"Open it anyway."

The envelope said callfortickets.com and had a return address in the city. Albert opened it to find two tickets. "Montreal at Toronto" was printed in bold letters.

"They're for Saturday's game!" he exclaimed.

"We can catch the four o'clock bus," his mother said. "We'll have to take our supper with us. We'll get home late, but—"

"Are we really going?"

Albert's mother crossed her arms on her chest and leaned back in her chair. "You're holding the tickets, aren't you?"

The day after tomorrow they'd be riding the bus along the big highway to the city. To the loud, teeming streets, the sports centre near the lake, lit up like a castle, just like you could see on *Hockey Night in Canada*. Albert had never been inside a real hockey arena or seen professional players up close. But the day after tomorrow he'd be there, cheering for his favourite team. And Lorne Cuddy, the best centre in the league, the best player ever, would lead the Leafs and trounce Montreal, and Albert would kid his—

A sinking feeling pushed aside Albert's excitement.

"Mom, you don't even like hockey."

She shrugged. "I don't know, it might be fun," she said without conviction.

"Grandad bought the tickets, didn't he?"

"He sent for them a month ago. They got here last week. He saved up for almost a year."

"For a rainy day," Albert whispered.

Albert paused outside his grandfather's door. He heard the double *clink* of the Zippo and the rustle of a newspaper being opened. He knocked.

The room was just big enough to hold a single bed, dresser and night table with a small lamp. The old man was sitting on the bed, pillows at his back, reading the paper. He lowered it, took the cigarette from his mouth and tapped it on the edge of the ashtray on the table.

"You look a little glum," he said.

Albert searched for words and couldn't find the ones he wanted. He stood silently for a moment.

"I'm sorry," he managed.

Slowly, his grandfather closed the newspaper and folded it twice. He raised his cigarette to his thin lips. In his other hand, he turned the Zippo over and over.

"You was ashamed of me," he said. "At the beer store that day."

"No! No, I wasn't!" Albert protested. Again, he rummaged for the right words. To explain. To justify. And once more the words fled before he found them.

He *had* been ashamed.

But only for an instant. Only because those guys in the shiny red diesel were laughing at his grandfather. At Albert, too, sitting in the beat-up truck, eyes fixed on the empty socket in the dashboard. How could he describe the sudden realization, the knowledge that came like a sharp pain, that so much was closed off from him? That he loved the old man holding up the line in the beer store, yet for that brief flash of time hadn't wanted people to know he was with him?

Albert stared at the counterpane at the foot of the bed. "I'm sorry," he said again.

"I wish I could tell you," his grandfather said, "that someday, if you work real hard, you'll live in a big house and drive a fancy new car and have lots of money in your jeans, but I can't. Maybe it'll happen, maybe it won't." The old man took a last long drag from his cigarette and stubbed it out in the ashtray. "That's just the way things are," he said.

"Grandad," Albert said. "I don't want to go to the game if you're not going."

The old man picked up the newspaper and unfolded it. He shook it open, turned a page, held it up to cover his face.

"Says here," he began, "that Cuddy could break the scoring record Saturday night. That would mean another record for those damn Maple Leafs, wouldn't it?"

"Yup," Albert said.

"Well, I guess I better go along to the game and make sure that doesn't happen."

acknowledgements

Thanks to Maya Mavjee for supporting this project; to my editor, Amy Black; to Shaun Oakey for his usual excellent copy edit; to Molly Macdonald for putting us up in Edinburgh and helping with historical background for "The Promise"; and, as always, to Ting-xing Ye for endless help and encouragement.

Alma

Times have been tough since Alma's father died and she and her mother had to give up the family farm and move into town. With few friends, Alma loves to lose herself in stories—books she reads and re-reads, and tales she writes herself.

To help make ends meet, Alma takes a job transcribing the letters of Miss Lily, the eccentric and reclusive elderly woman who has just moved into the old house on Little Wharf Road.

Eventually, their mutual love of words creates a strong relationship, and Miss Lily encourages Alma's spark for writing, introducing her to the art of calligraphy and lending her some of her favourite books. But why is Miss Lily so secretive about certain parts of her life?

Alma is determined to find out—but will she be prepared for what she will discover? . . .

Stones

Garnet Havelock know what it's like to be on the outside, not one of the crowd. Now, in his final year of high school, he's just marking time, waiting to get out into the real world.

Then a mysterious girl transfers to his school and Garnet thinks he might have found the woman of his dreams—if only he could get her to talk to him.

At the same time, Garnet becomes caught up in a mystery centred in his community. As he and Raphaella draw closer to the truth, they uncover a horrifying chapter in the town's history, and learn how deep-seated prejudices and persecution from the past can still reverberate in the present.